MW01580494

SERVICE PUPS in Training

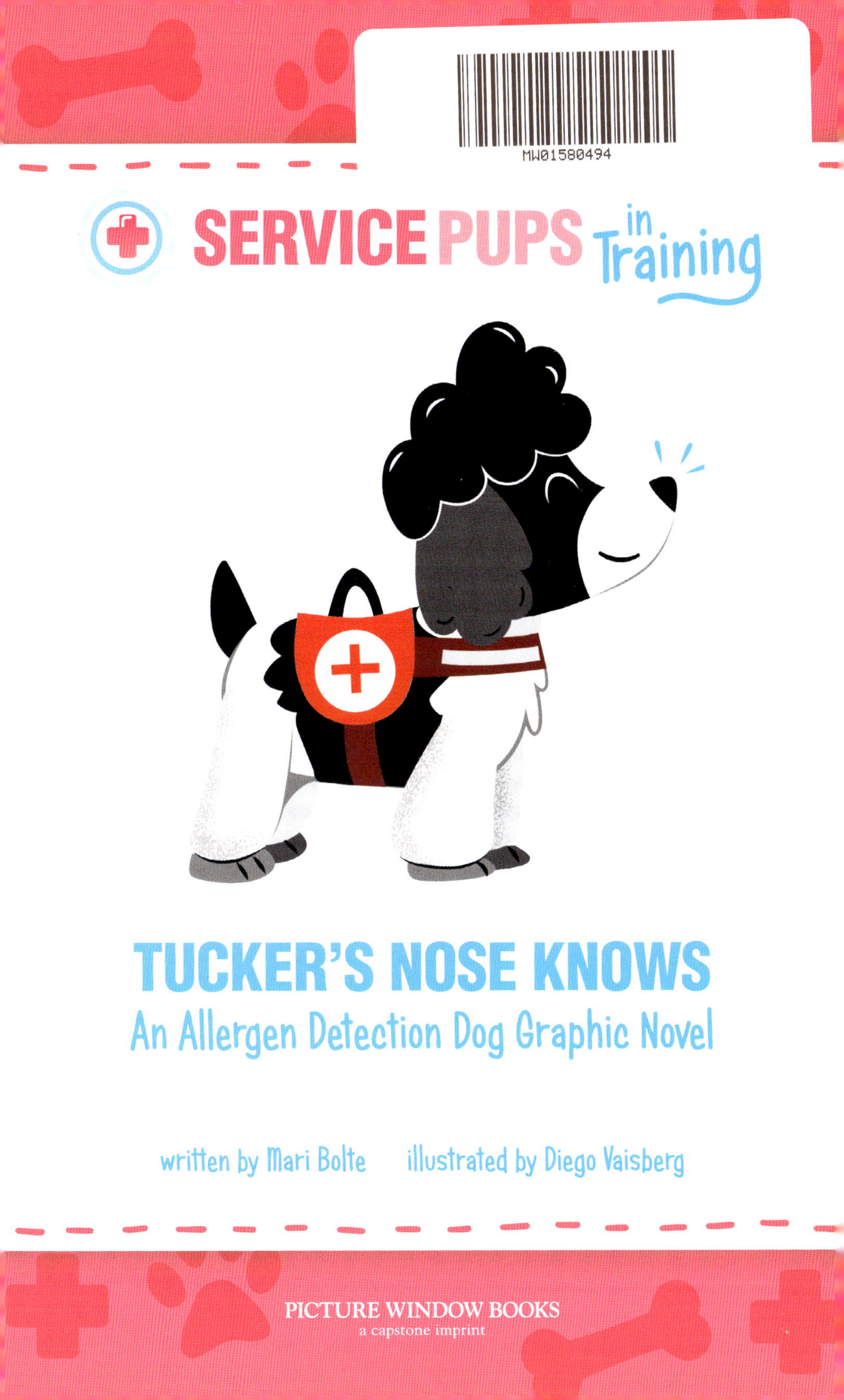

TUCKER'S NOSE KNOWS

An Allergen Detection Dog Graphic Novel

written by Mari Bolte illustrated by Diego Vaisberg

PICTURE WINDOW BOOKS
a capstone imprint

Published by Picture Window Books, an imprint of Capstone
1710 Roe Crest Drive, North Mankato, Minnesota 56003
www.capstonepub.com

Copyright © 2024 by Capstone. All rights reserved. No part of this publication may be reproduced in whole or in part, or stored in a retrieval system, or transmitted in any form or by any means, electronic, mechanical, photocopying, recording, or otherwise, without written permission of the publisher.

Library of Congress Cataloging-in-Publication Data
Names: Bolte, Mari, author. | Vaisberg, Diego, illustrator.
Title: Tucker's nose knows : an allergy detection dog graphic novel / by Mari Bolte ; illustrated by Diego Vaisberg.
Description: North Mankato, Minnesota : Picture Window Books, [2024] | Series: Service pups in training | Audience: Ages 5 to 7 | Audience: Grades 2-3 | Summary: Tucker is a poodle training to become an allergy detection dog — strong, calm, hypoallergenic, and a good listener.
Identifiers: LCCN 2022044546 (print) | LCCN 2022044547 (ebook) | ISBN 9781484680186 (hardcover) | ISBN 9781484680131 (paperback) | ISBN 9781484680148 (pdf) | ISBN 781484680162 (kindle edition) | ISBN 9781484680179 (epub) Subjects: CYAC: Graphic novels. | Poodles—Fiction. | Dogs—Fiction. | Service dogs—Training—Fiction. | Allergy—Fiction. | LCGFT: Animal fiction. | Graphic novels. Classification: LCC PZ7.7.B64 Tu 2024 (print) | LCC PZ7.7.B64 (ebook) | DDC 741.5/973—dc23/eng/20230209
LC record available at https://lccn.loc.gov/2022044546
LC ebook record available at https://lccn.loc.gov/2022044547

Editorial Credits
Editor: Christianne Jones; Designer: Elyse White; Media Researcher: Rebekah Hubstenberger; Production Specialist: Whitney Schaefer

Image and Design Credits
Shutterstock: Debra Anderson, 30, minizen, design element (bone icon)

Meet Tucker

Tucker is a poodle training to become an allergen detection dog. Poodles are considered to be hypoallergenic. That means they are less likely to cause allergic reactions. This makes them good for people who have pet allergies. They are strong and fast but are also calm and listen well. Tucker loves going to the groomer and stopping for a pup cup afterward.

How to Read a GRAPHIC NOVEL

Graphic novels are easy to read. Boxes called panels show you how to follow the story. Look at the panels from left to right and top to bottom.

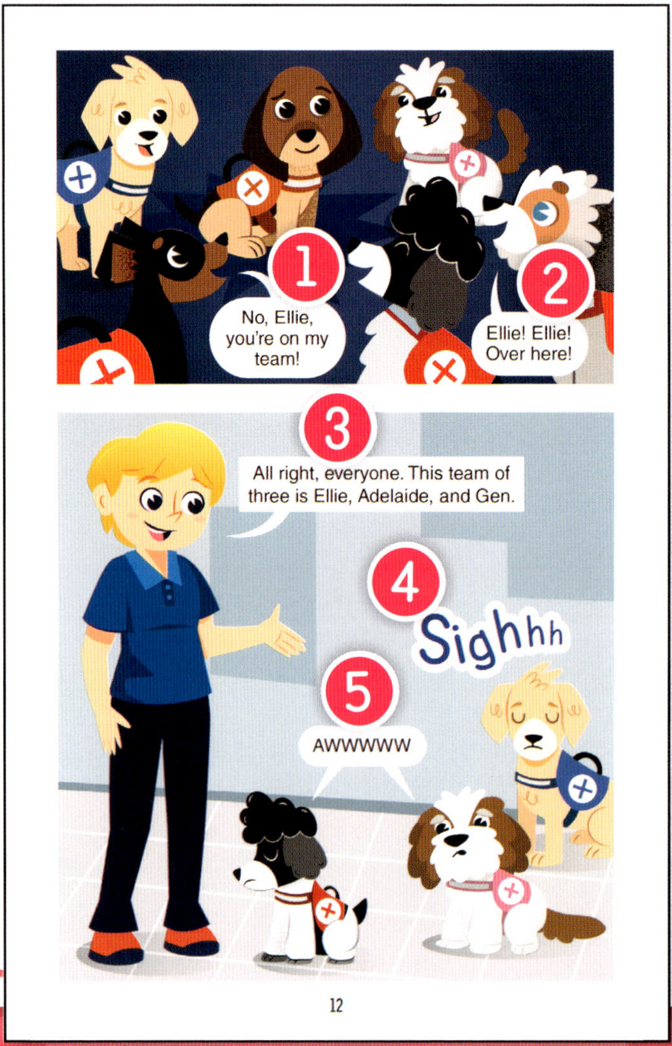
1
No, Ellie, you're on my team!
2
Ellie! Ellie! Over here!
3
All right, everyone. This team of three is Ellie, Adelaide, and Gen.
4
Sighhh
5
AWWWWWW
12

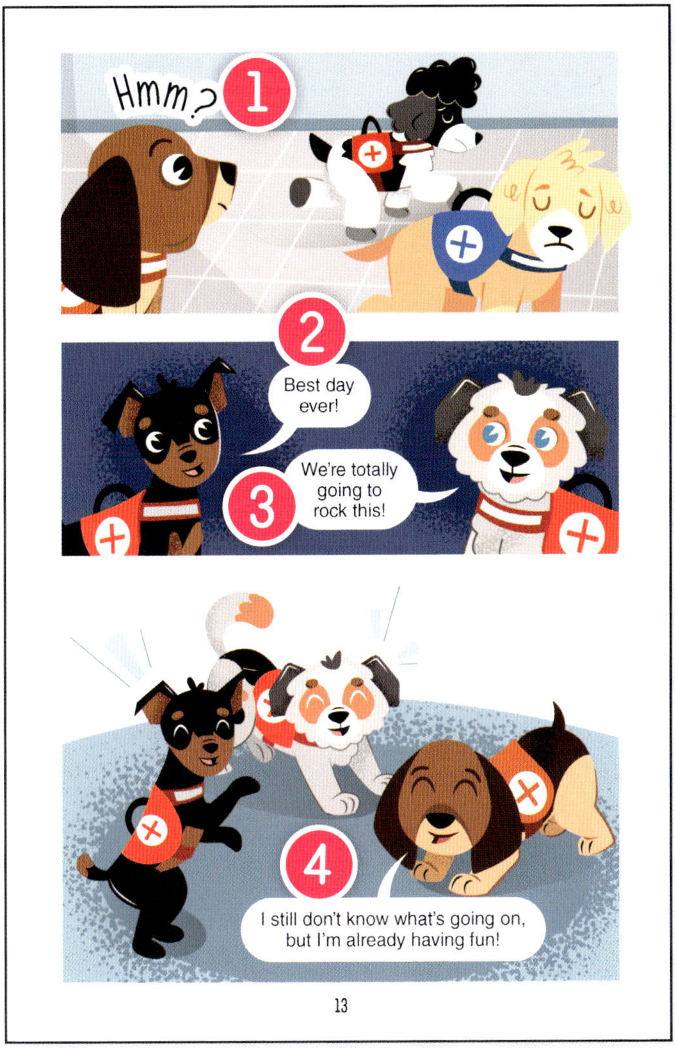
Hmm?
1
2
Best day ever!
3
We're totally going to rock this!
4
I still don't know what's going on, but I'm already having fun!
13

Read the word boxes and word balloons from left to right as well. Don't forget the sound and action words in the pictures. The pictures and the words work together to tell the whole story.

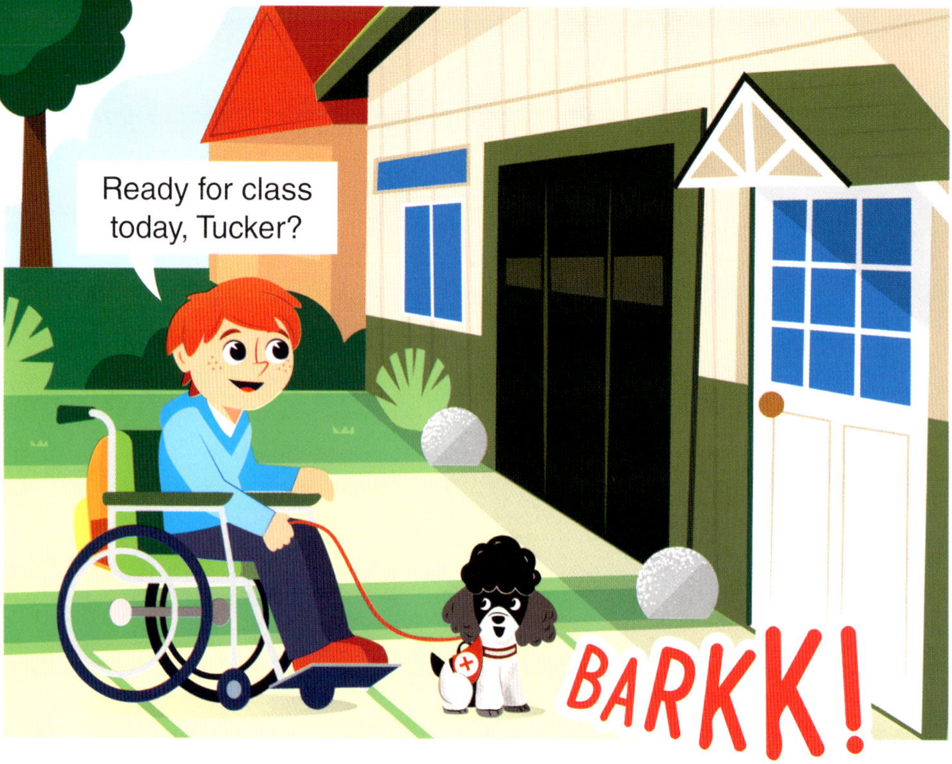
Ready for class today, Tucker?
BARKK!

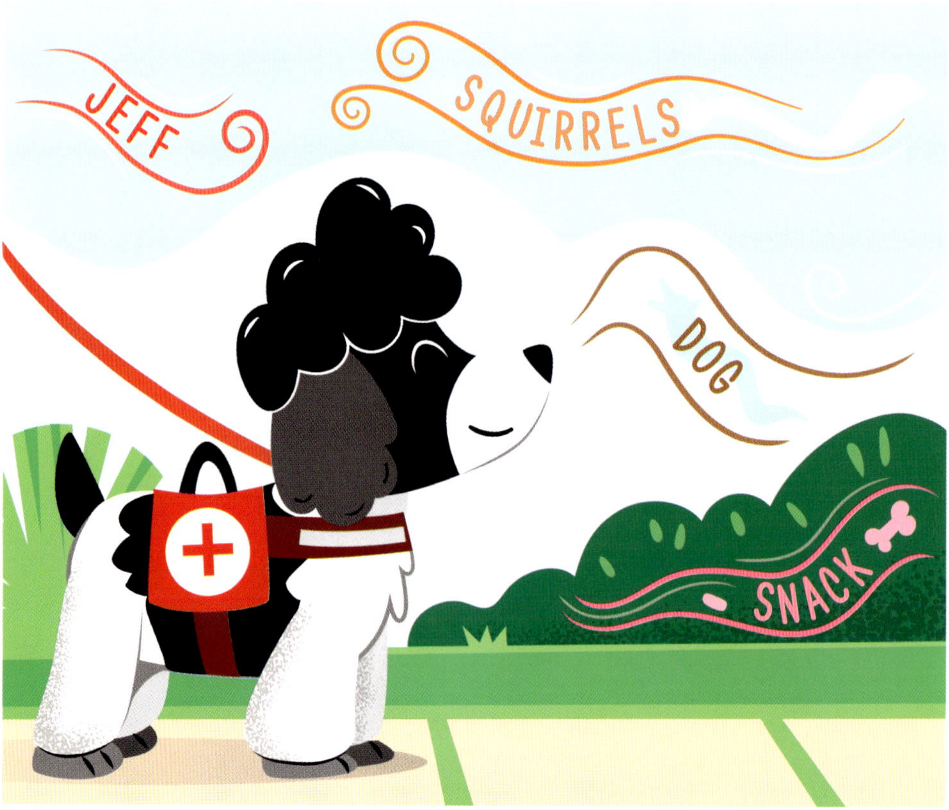
JEFF
SQUIRRELS
DOG
SNACK

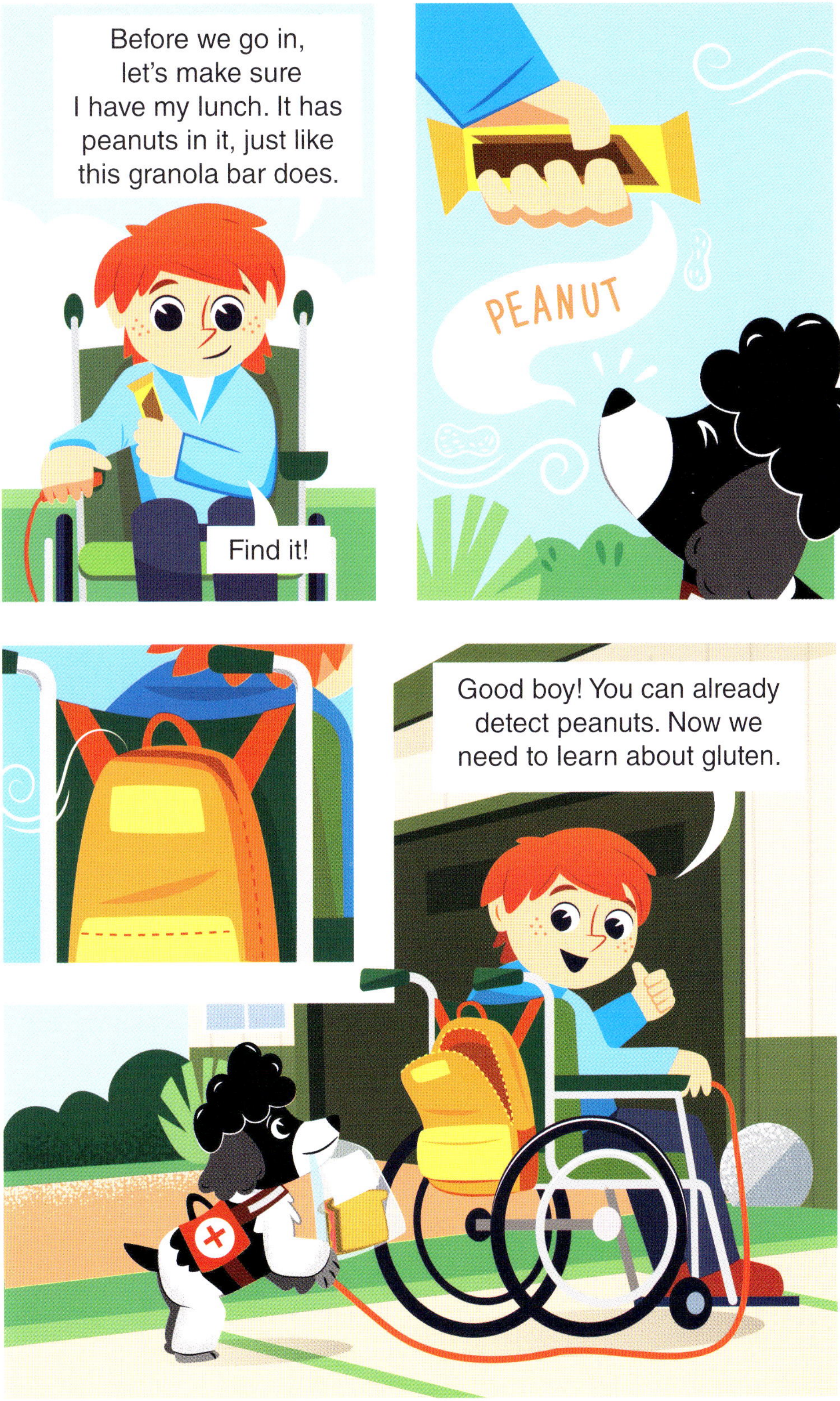
Before we go in, let's make sure I have my lunch. It has peanuts in it, just like this granola bar does.
Find it!
PEANUT
Good boy! You can already detect peanuts. Now we need to learn about gluten.

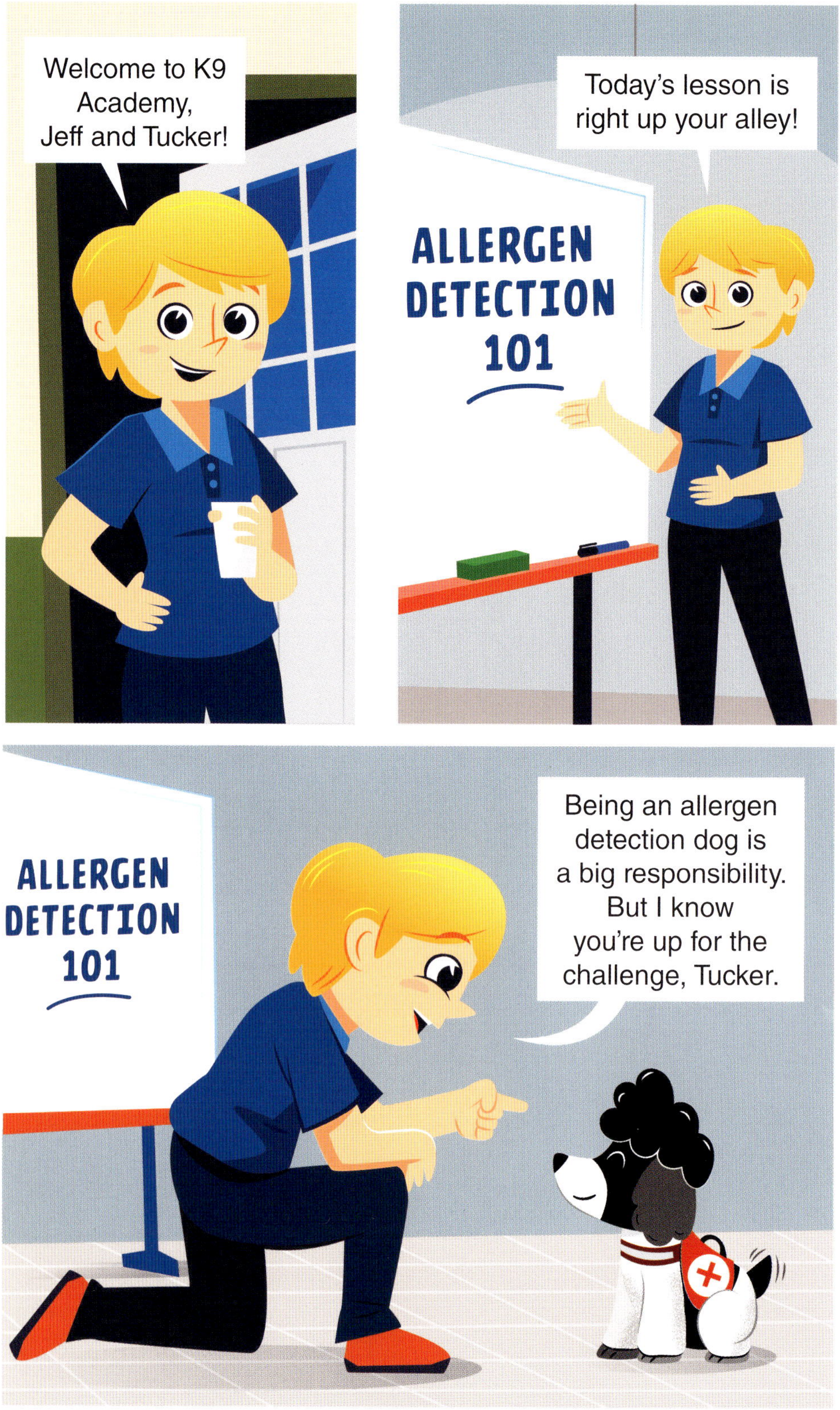

Welcome to K9 Academy, Jeff and Tucker!
Today's lesson is right up your alley!
ALLERGEN DETECTION 101
ALLERGEN DETECTION 101
Being an allergen detection dog is a big responsibility. But I know you're up for the challenge, Tucker.

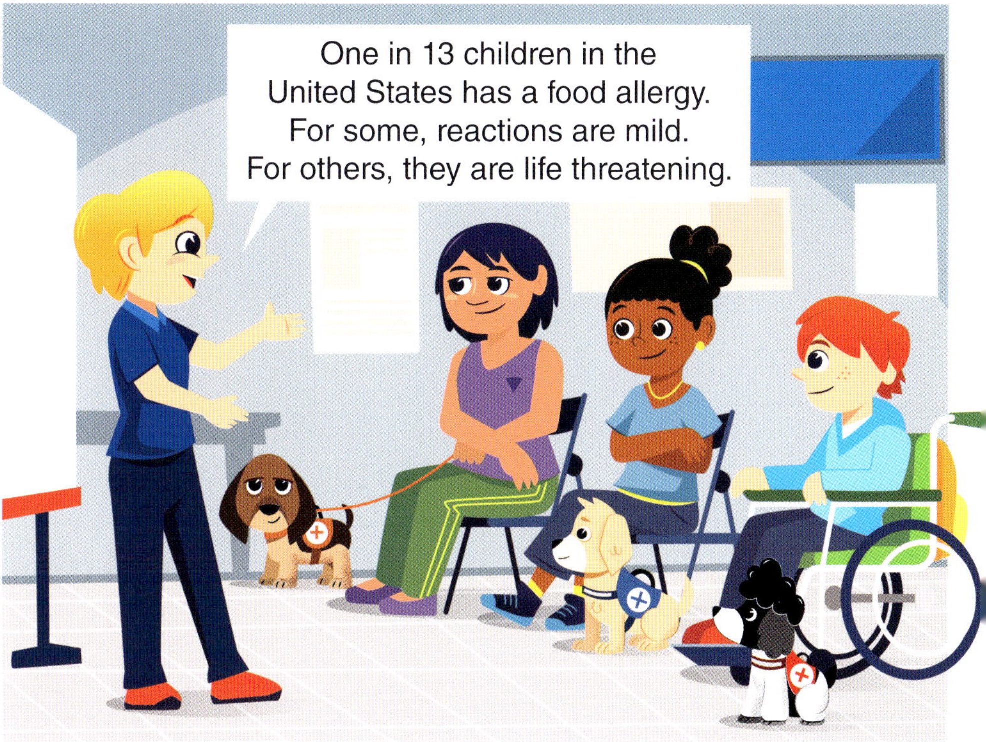
One in 13 children in the United States has a food allergy. For some, reactions are mild. For others, they are life threatening.

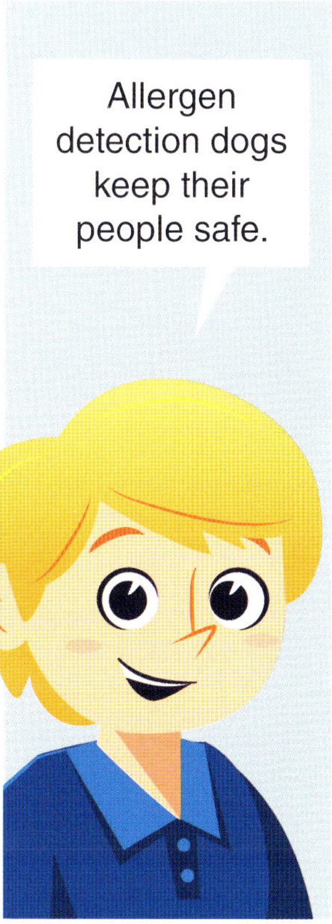
Allergen detection dogs keep their people safe.

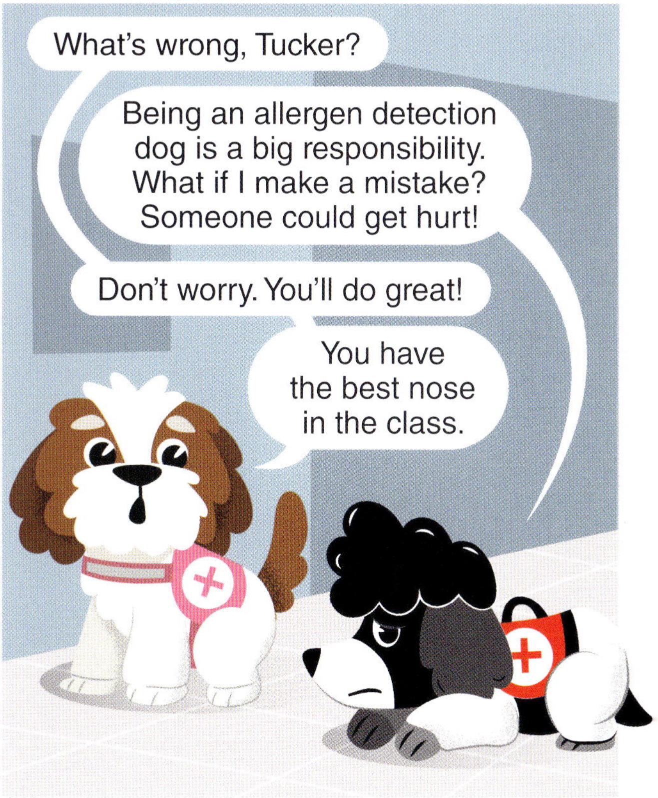
What's wrong, Tucker?
Being an allergen detection dog is a big responsibility. What if I make a mistake? Someone could get hurt!
Don't worry. You'll do great!
You have the best nose in the class.

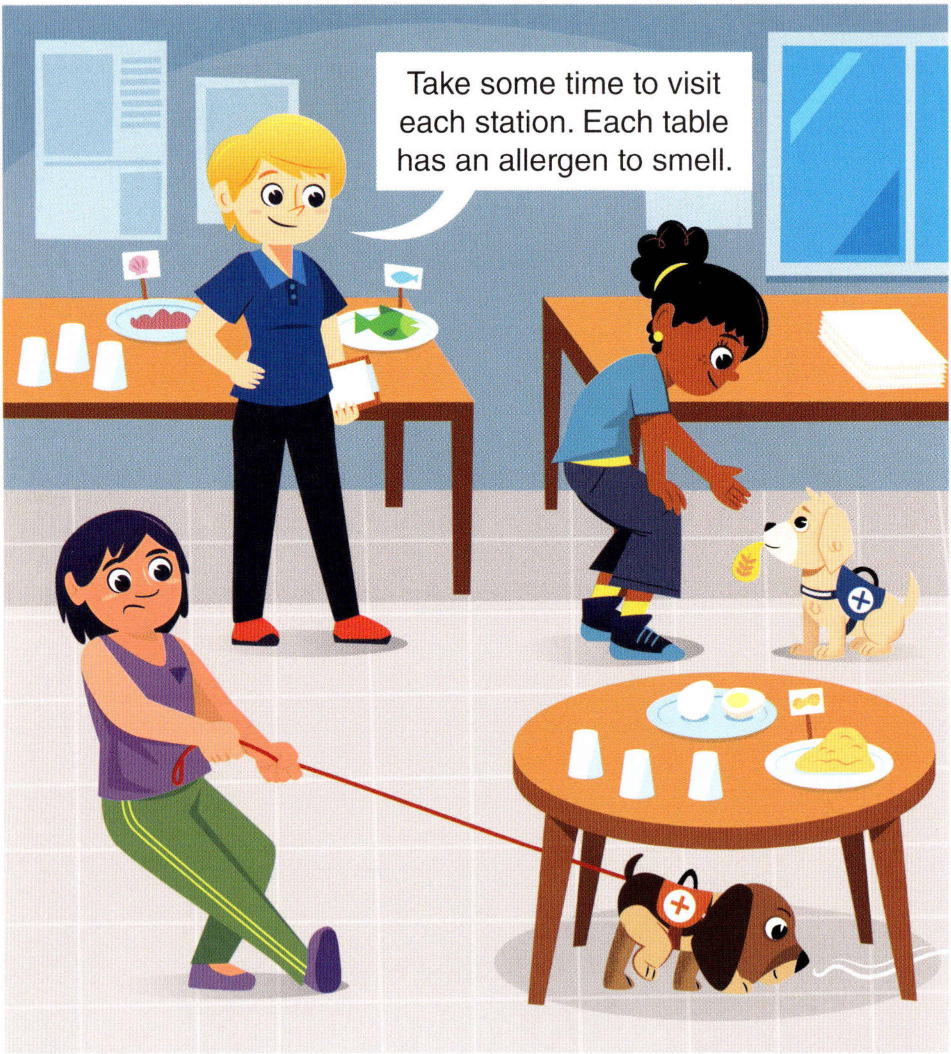
Take some time to visit each station. Each table has an allergen to smell.

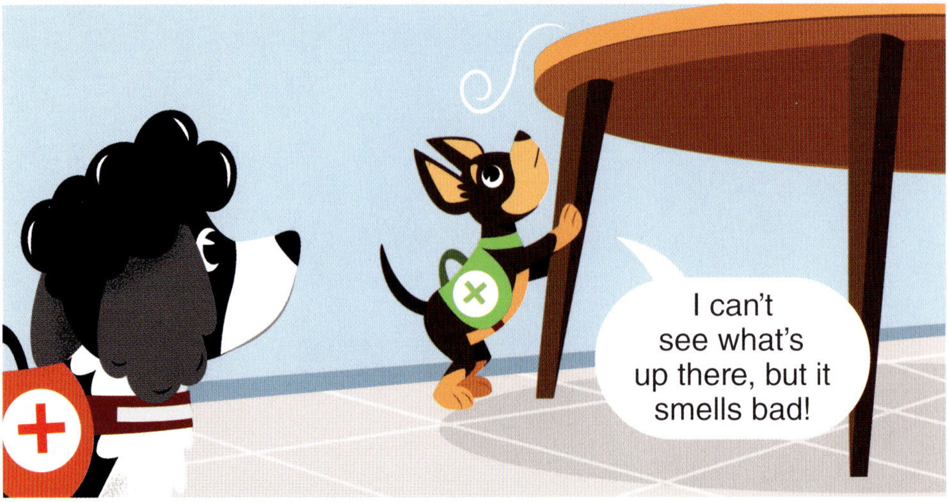
I can't see what's up there, but it smells bad!

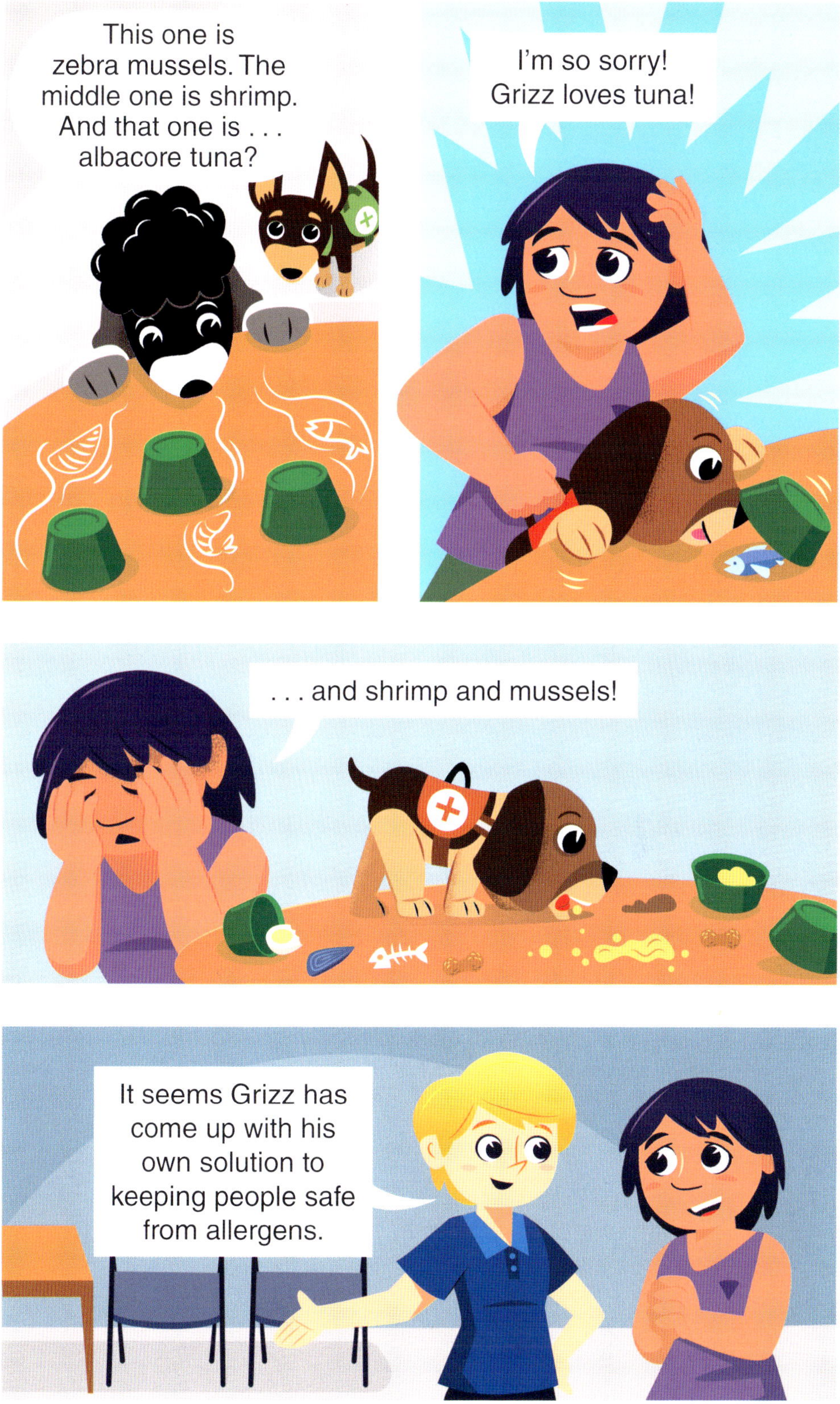
This one is zebra mussels. The middle one is shrimp. And that one is . . . albacore tuna?
I'm so sorry! Grizz loves tuna!
. . . and shrimp and mussels!
It seems Grizz has come up with his own solution to keeping people safe from allergens.

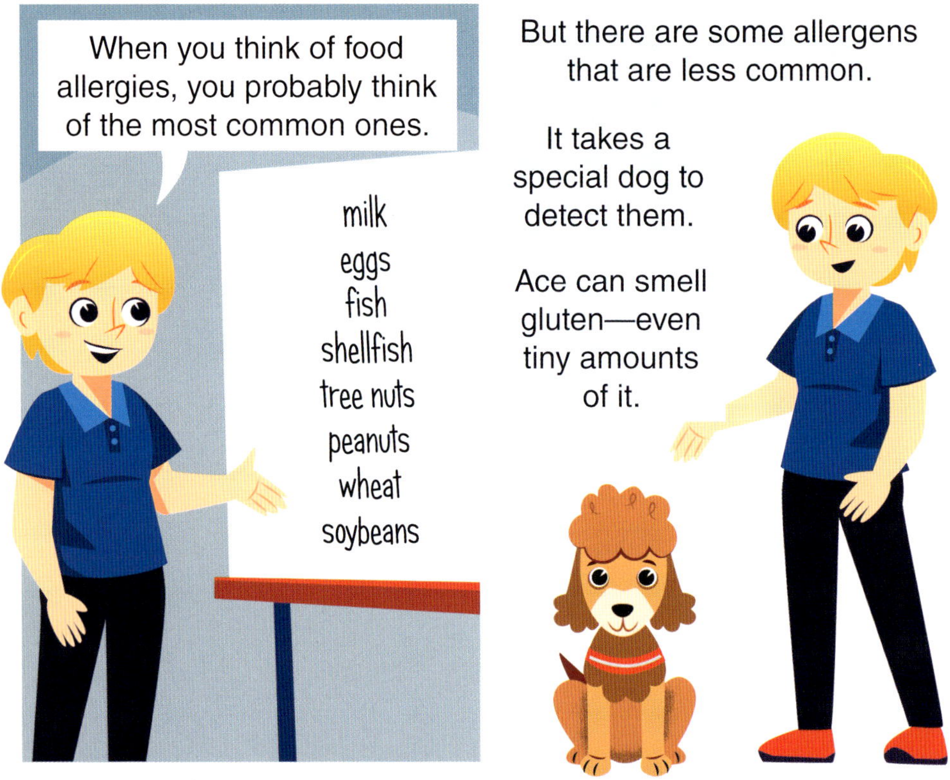
When you think of food allergies, you probably think of the most common ones.
milk
eggs
fish
shellfish
tree nuts
peanuts
wheat
soybeans
But there are some allergens that are less common.
It takes a special dog to detect them.
Ace can smell gluten—even tiny amounts of it.

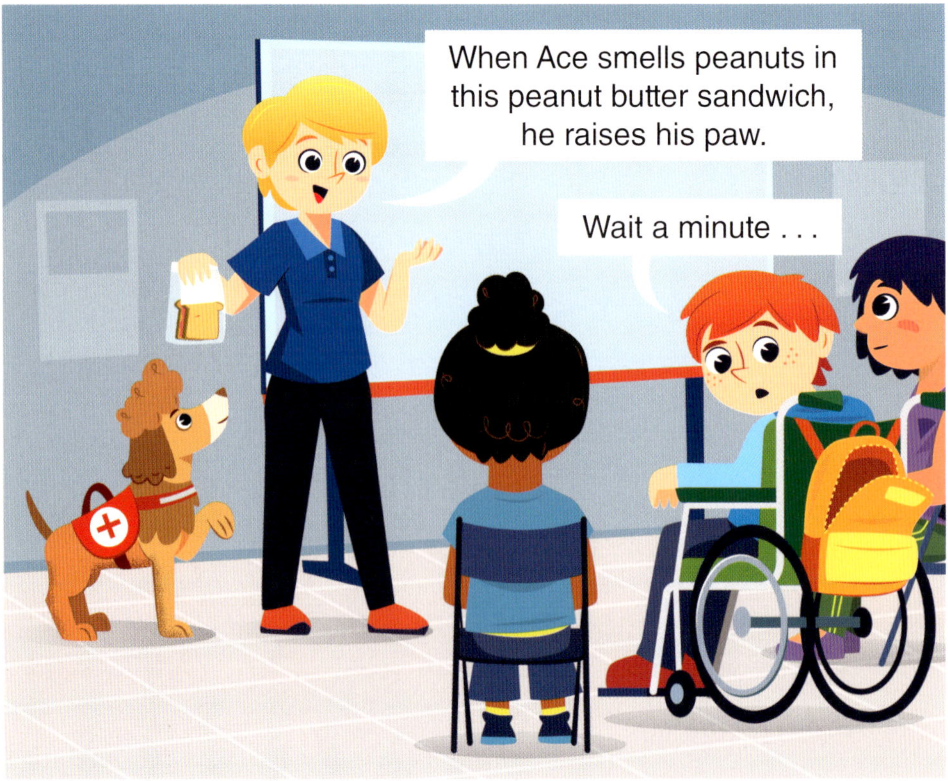
When Ace smells peanuts in this peanut butter sandwich, he raises his paw.
Wait a minute . . .

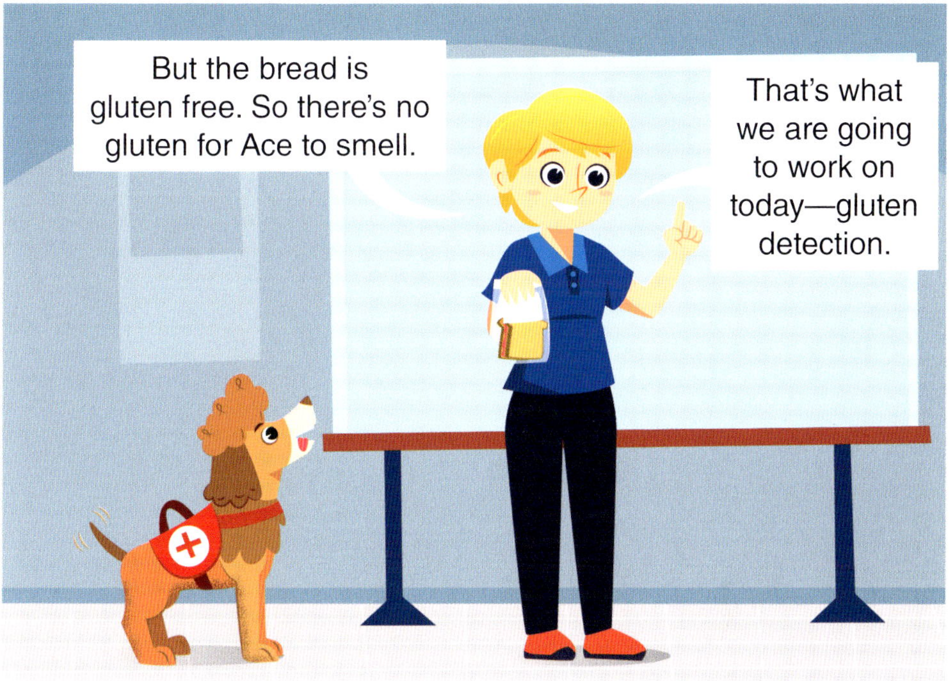
But the bread is gluten free. So there's no gluten for Ace to smell.
That's what we are going to work on today—gluten detection.

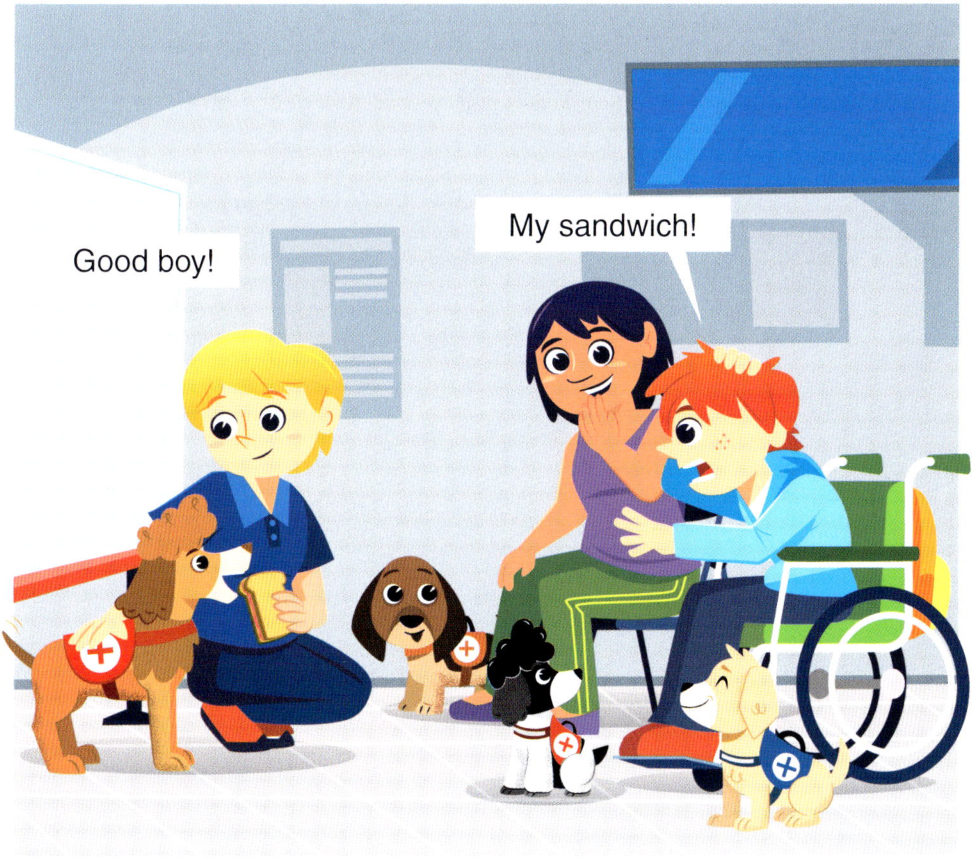
Good boy!
My sandwich!

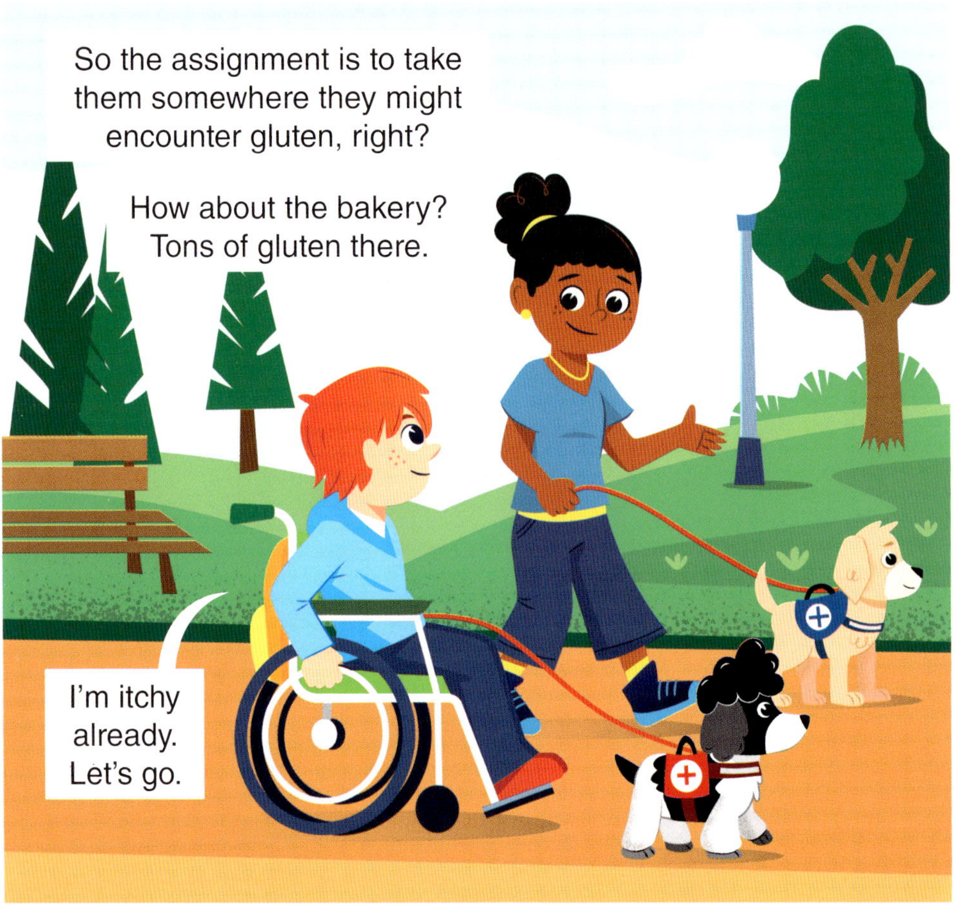
So the assignment is to take them somewhere they might encounter gluten, right?
How about the bakery? Tons of gluten there.
I'm itchy already. Let's go.

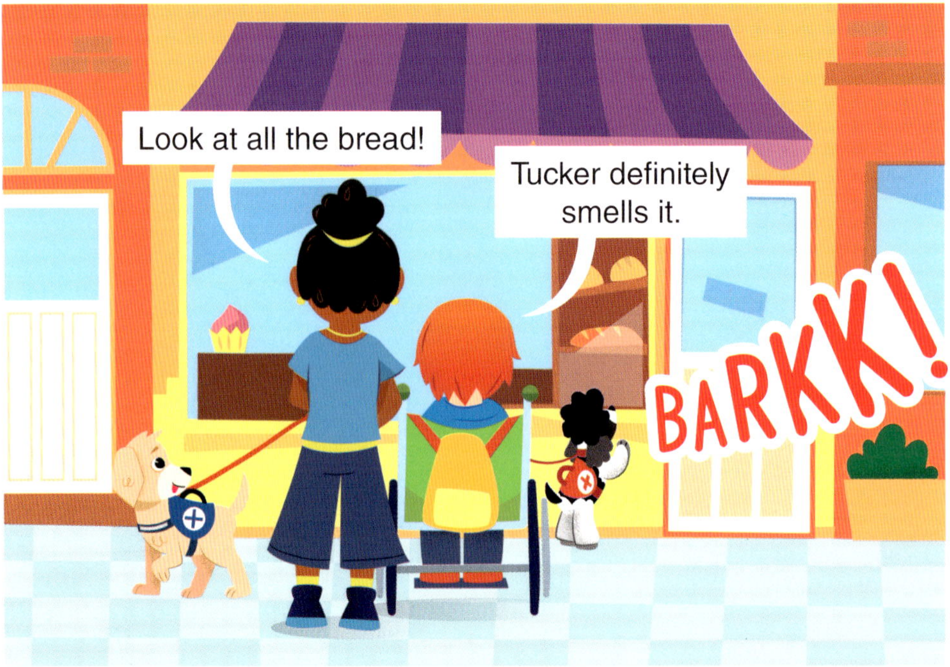
Look at all the bread!
Tucker definitely smells it.
BARKK!

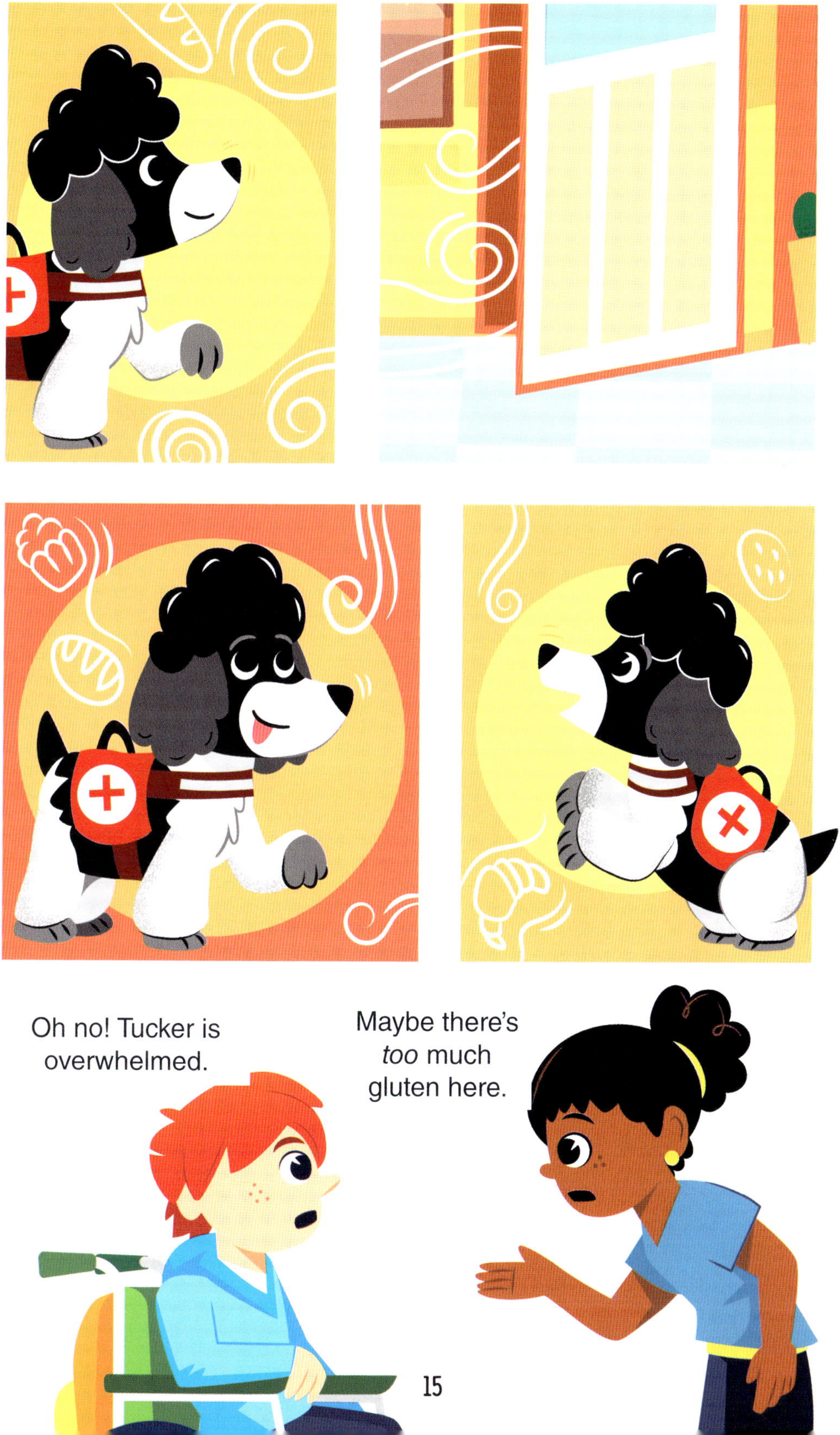

Oh no! Tucker is overwhelmed.
Maybe there's *too* much gluten here.

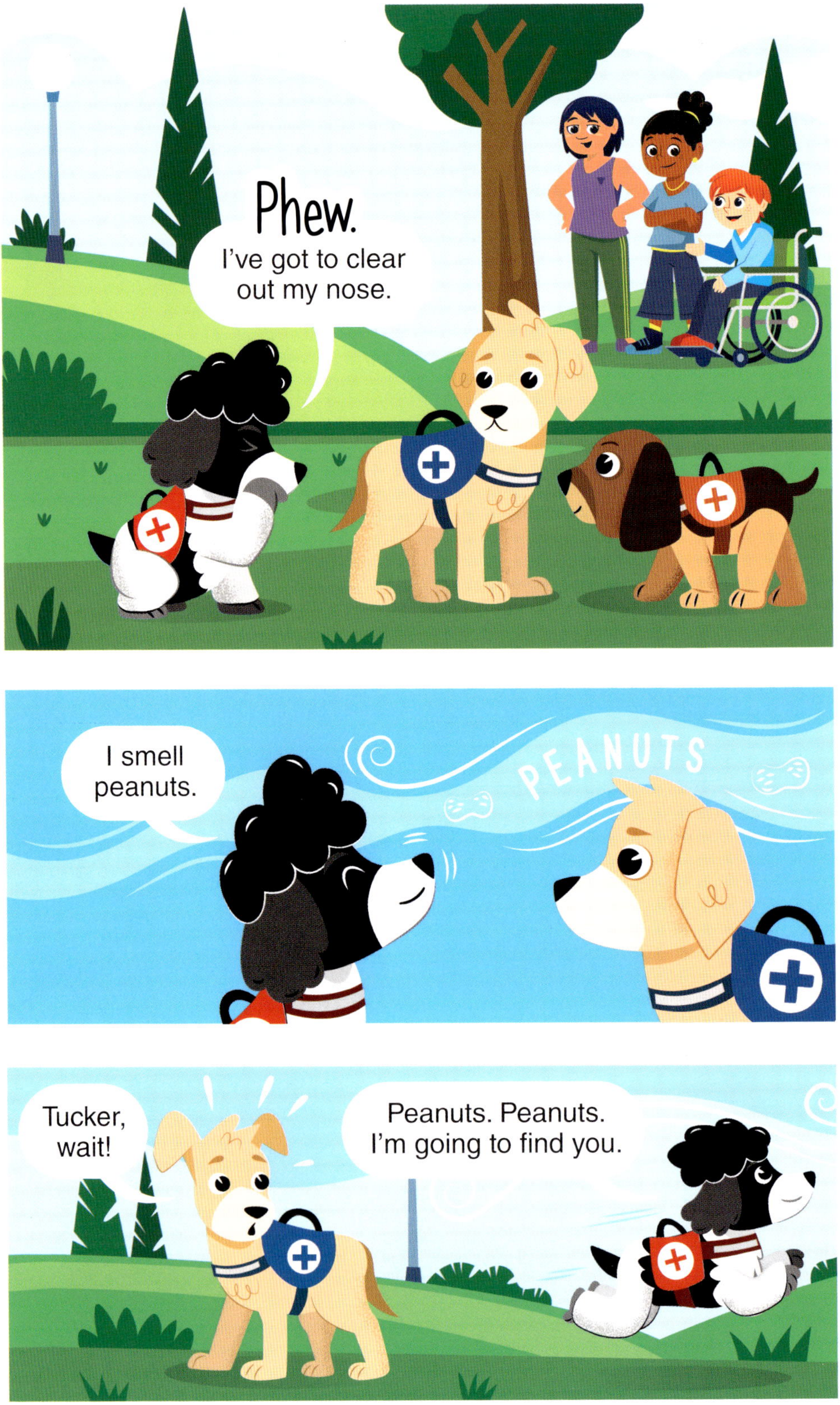
Phew.
I've got to clear out my nose.
I smell peanuts.
PEANUTS
Tucker, wait!
Peanuts. Peanuts. I'm going to find you.

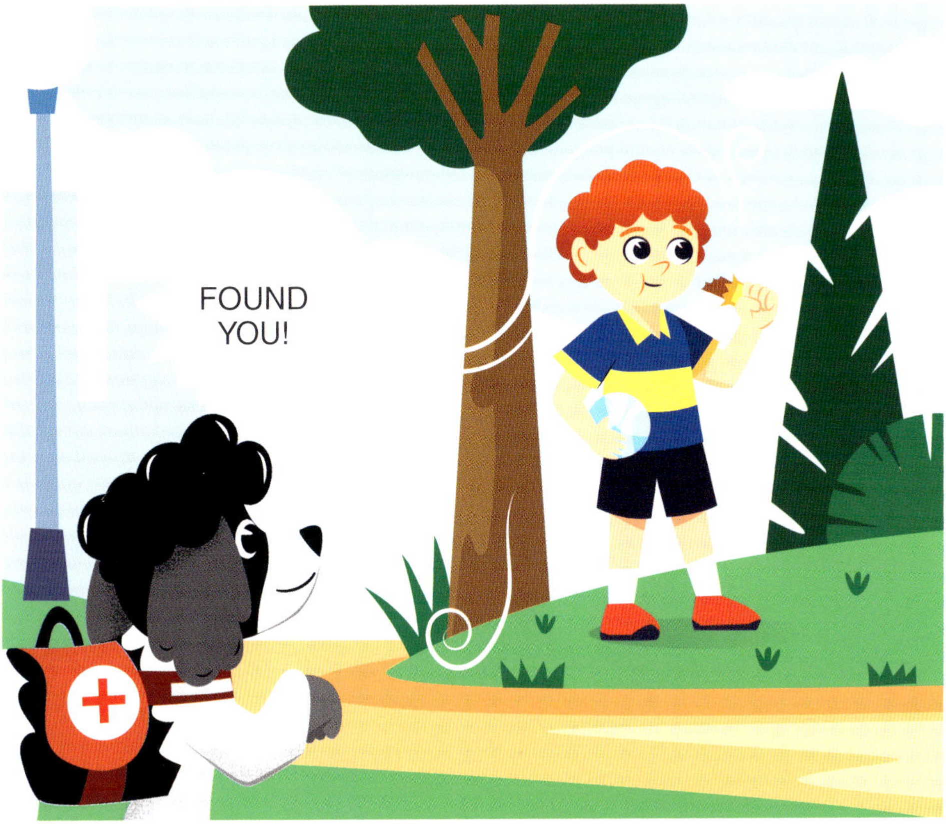
FOUND YOU!

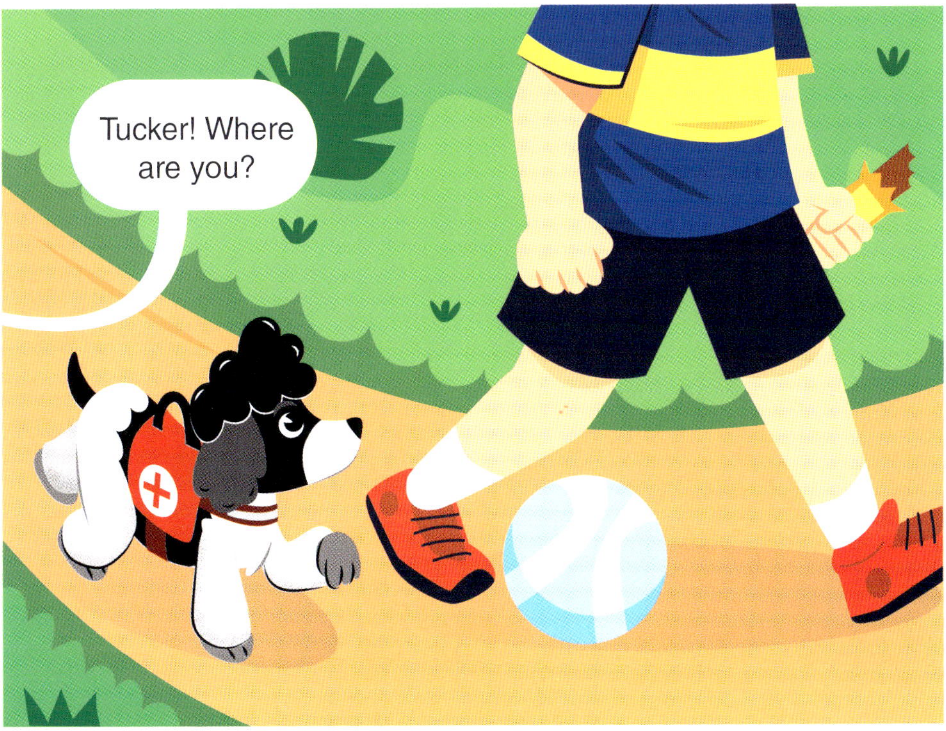
Tucker! Where are you?

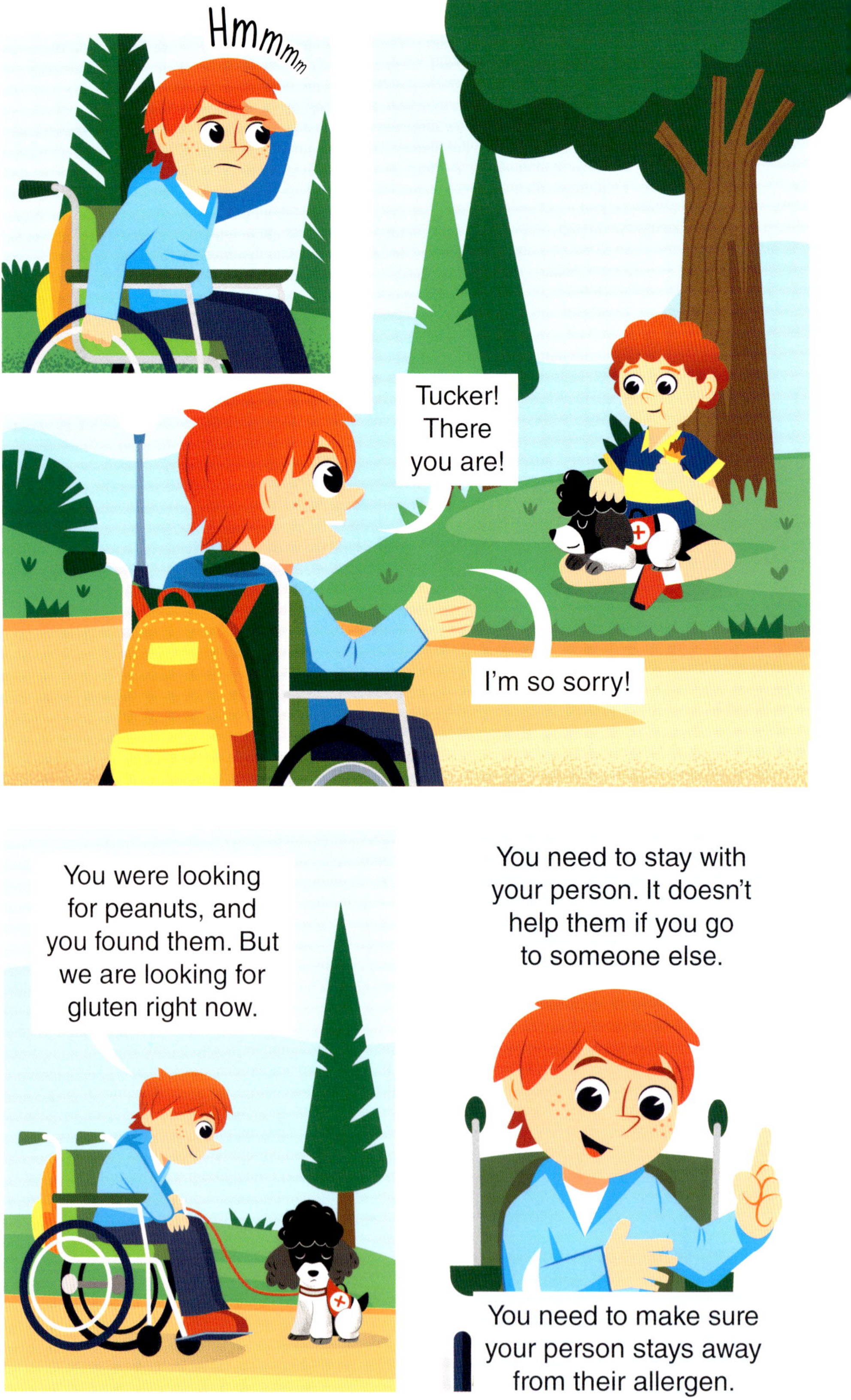
Hmmmm
Tucker! There you are!
I'm so sorry!
You were looking for peanuts, and you found them. But we are looking for gluten right now.
You need to stay with your person. It doesn't help them if you go to someone else.
You need to make sure your person stays away from their allergen.

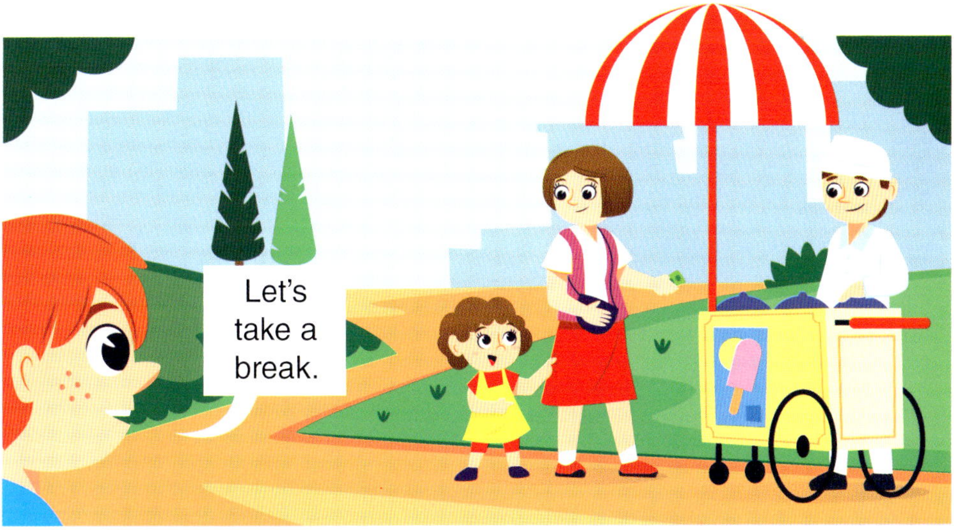
Let's take a break.

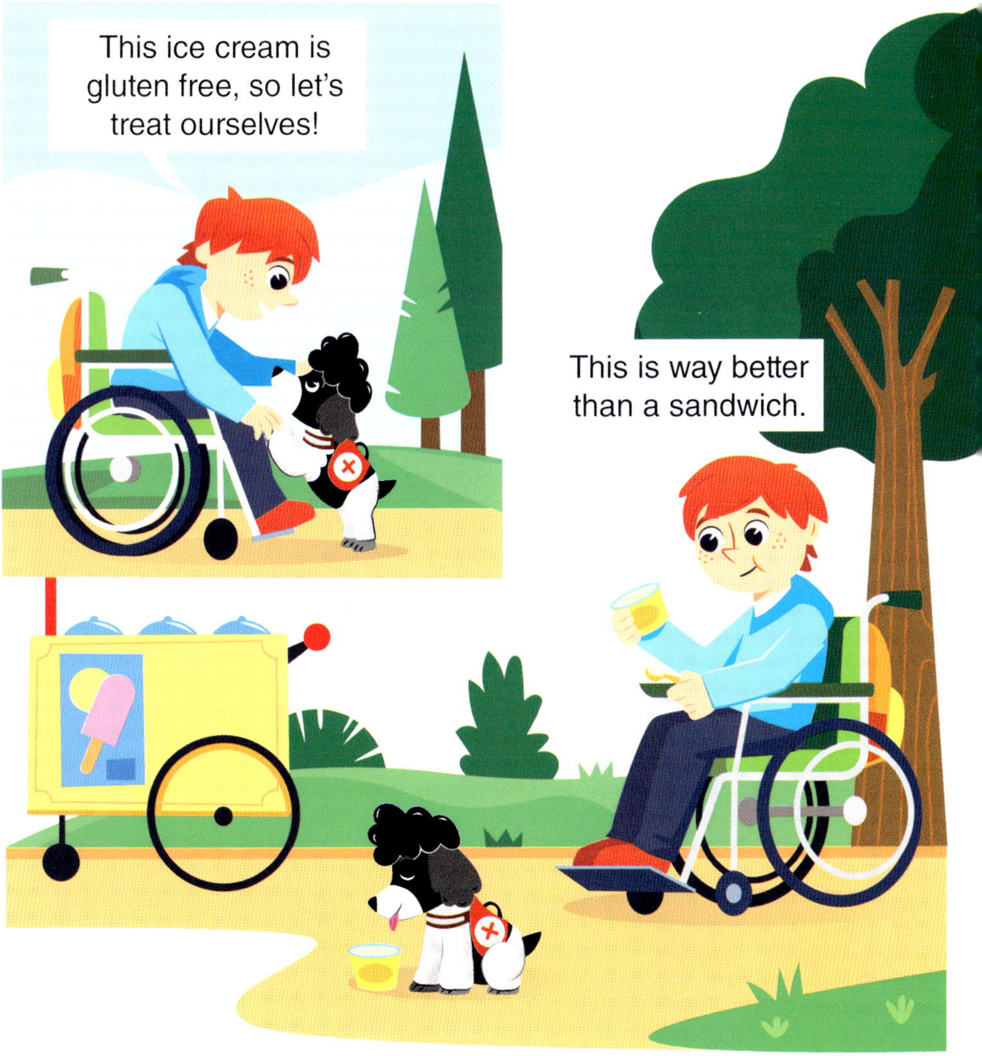
This ice cream is gluten free, so let's treat ourselves!
This is way better than a sandwich.

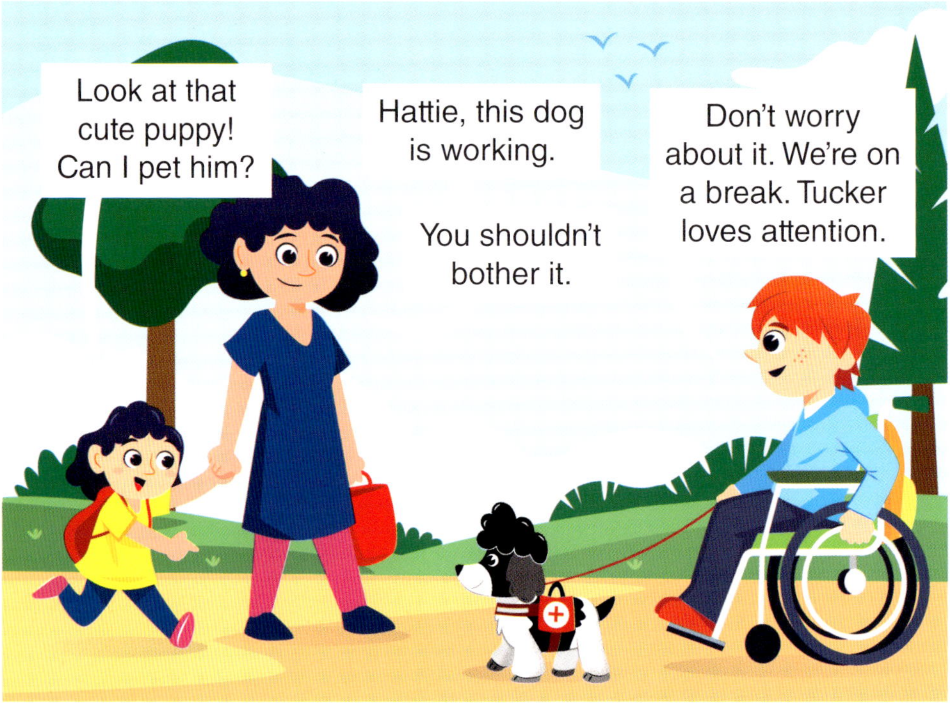
Look at that cute puppy! Can I pet him?
Hattie, this dog is working.
You shouldn't bother it.
Don't worry about it. We're on a break. Tucker loves attention.

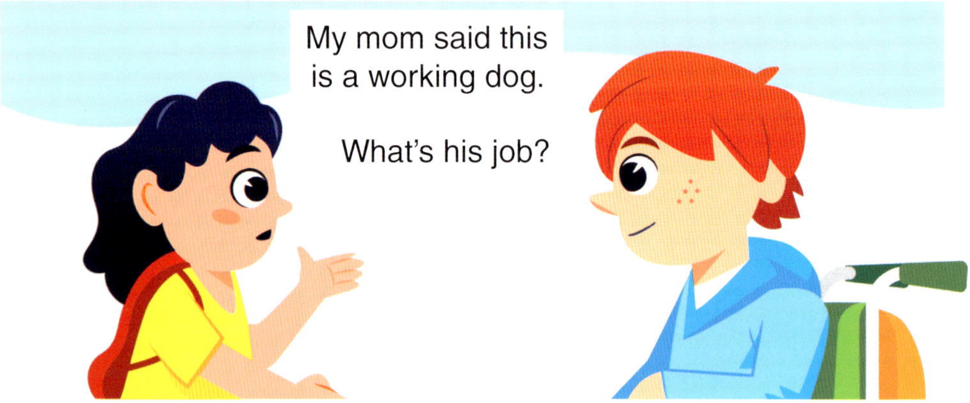
My mom said this is a working dog.
What's his job?

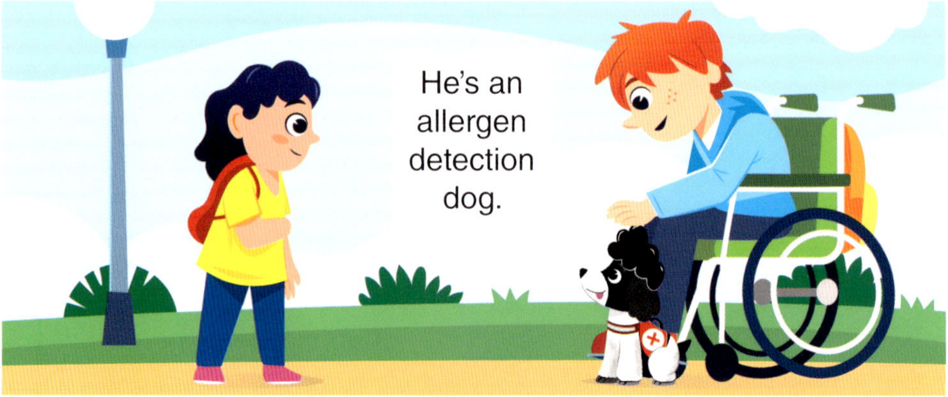
He's an allergen detection dog.

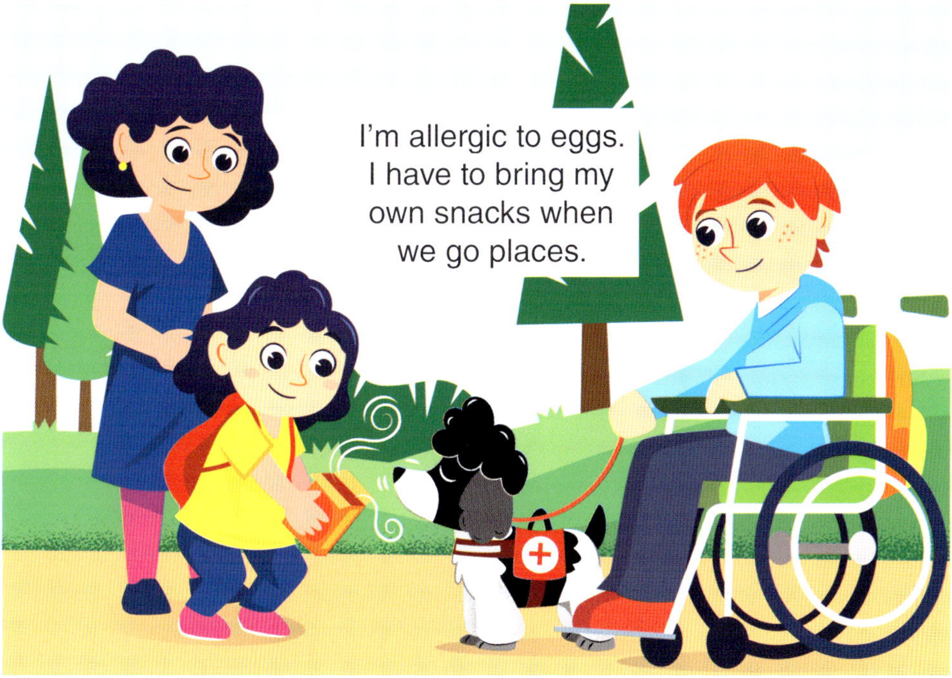
I'm allergic to eggs.
I have to bring my
own snacks when
we go places.

Maybe someday
I'll have a dog
just like him.

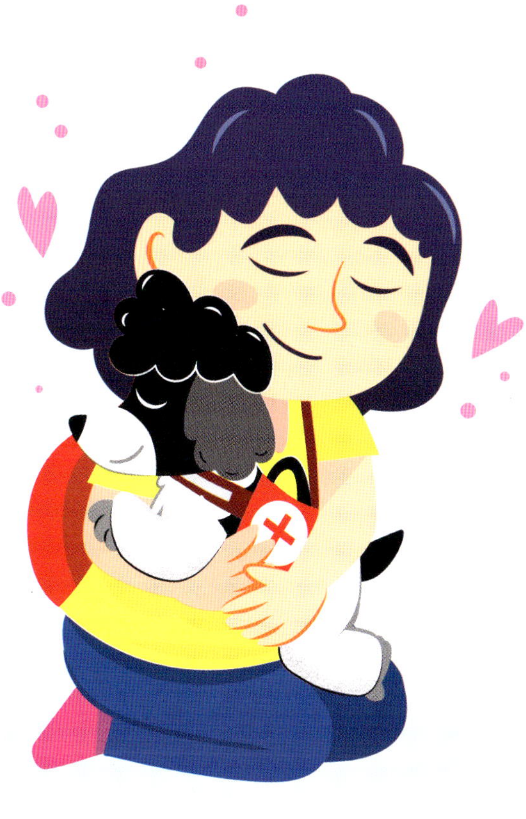

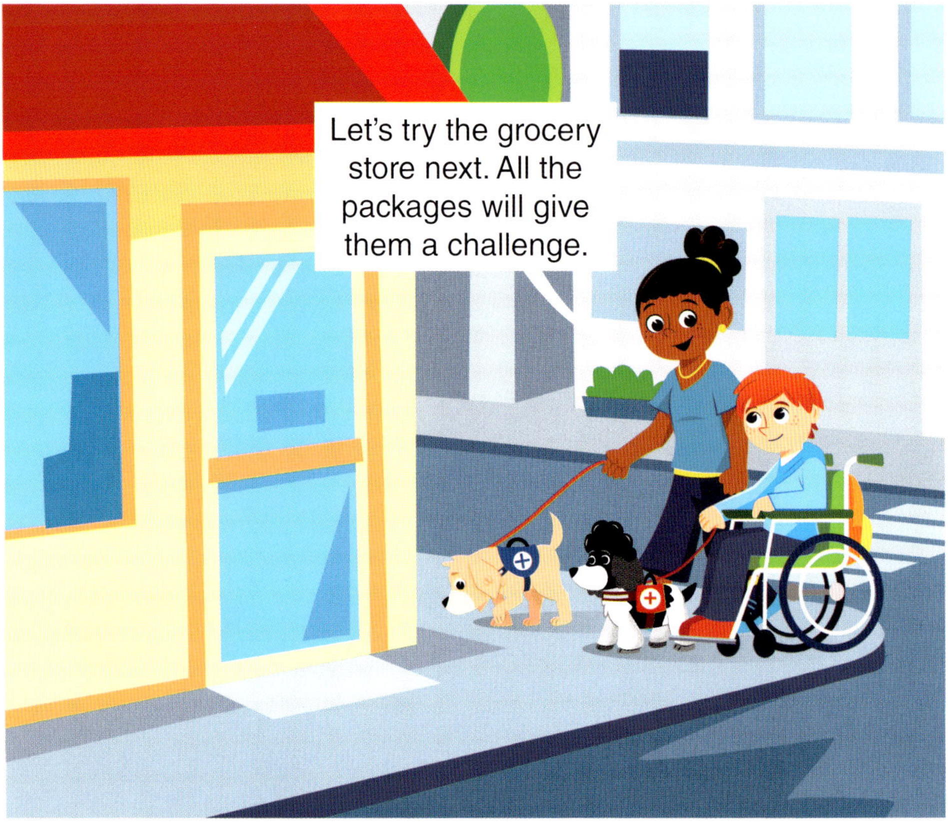
Let's try the grocery store next. All the packages will give them a challenge.

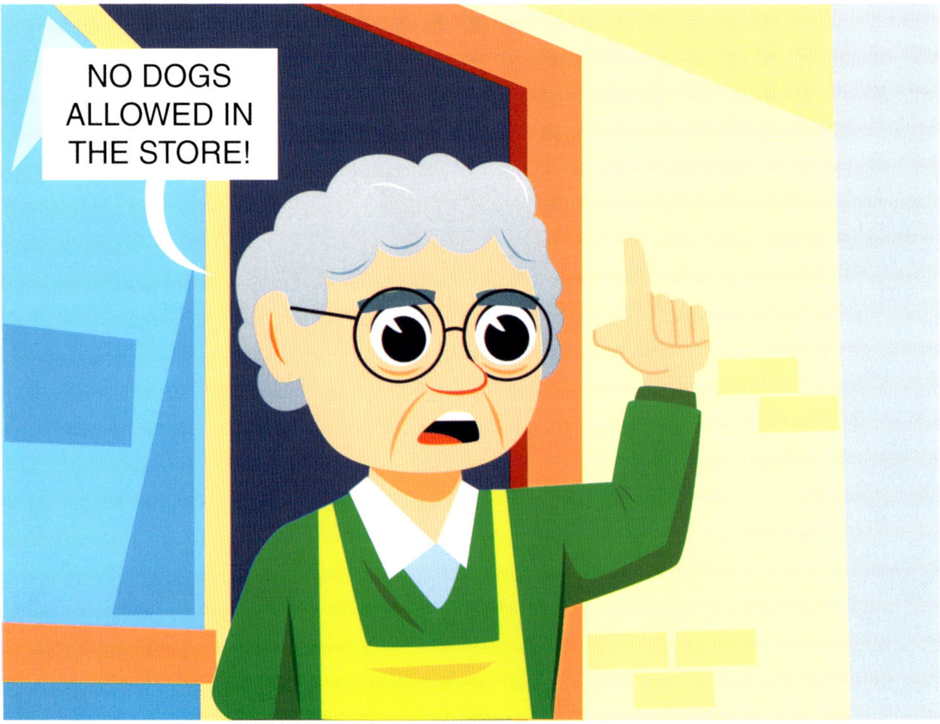
NO DOGS ALLOWED IN THE STORE!

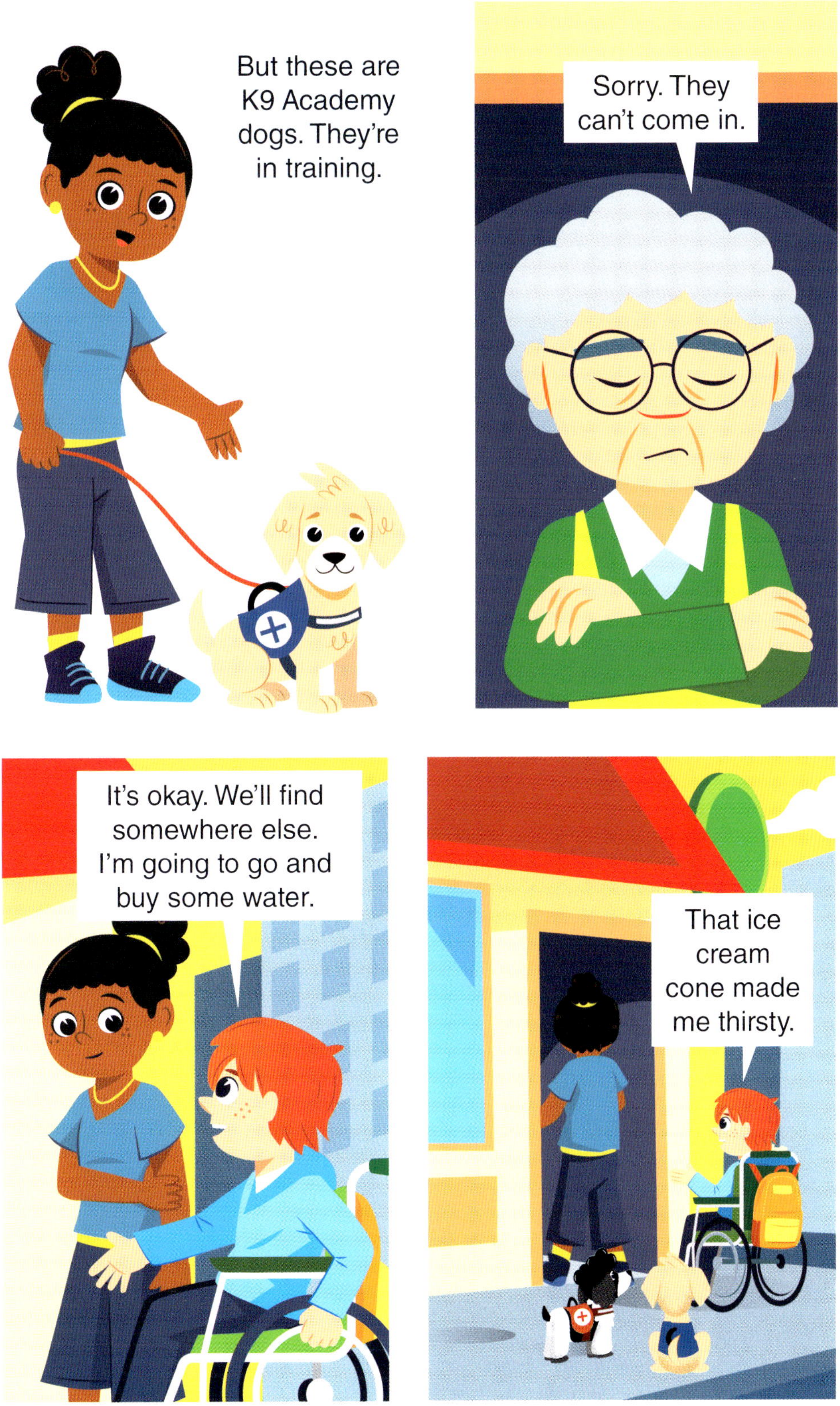
But these are K9 Academy dogs. They're in training.
Sorry. They can't come in.
It's okay. We'll find somewhere else. I'm going to go and buy some water.
That ice cream cone made me thirsty.

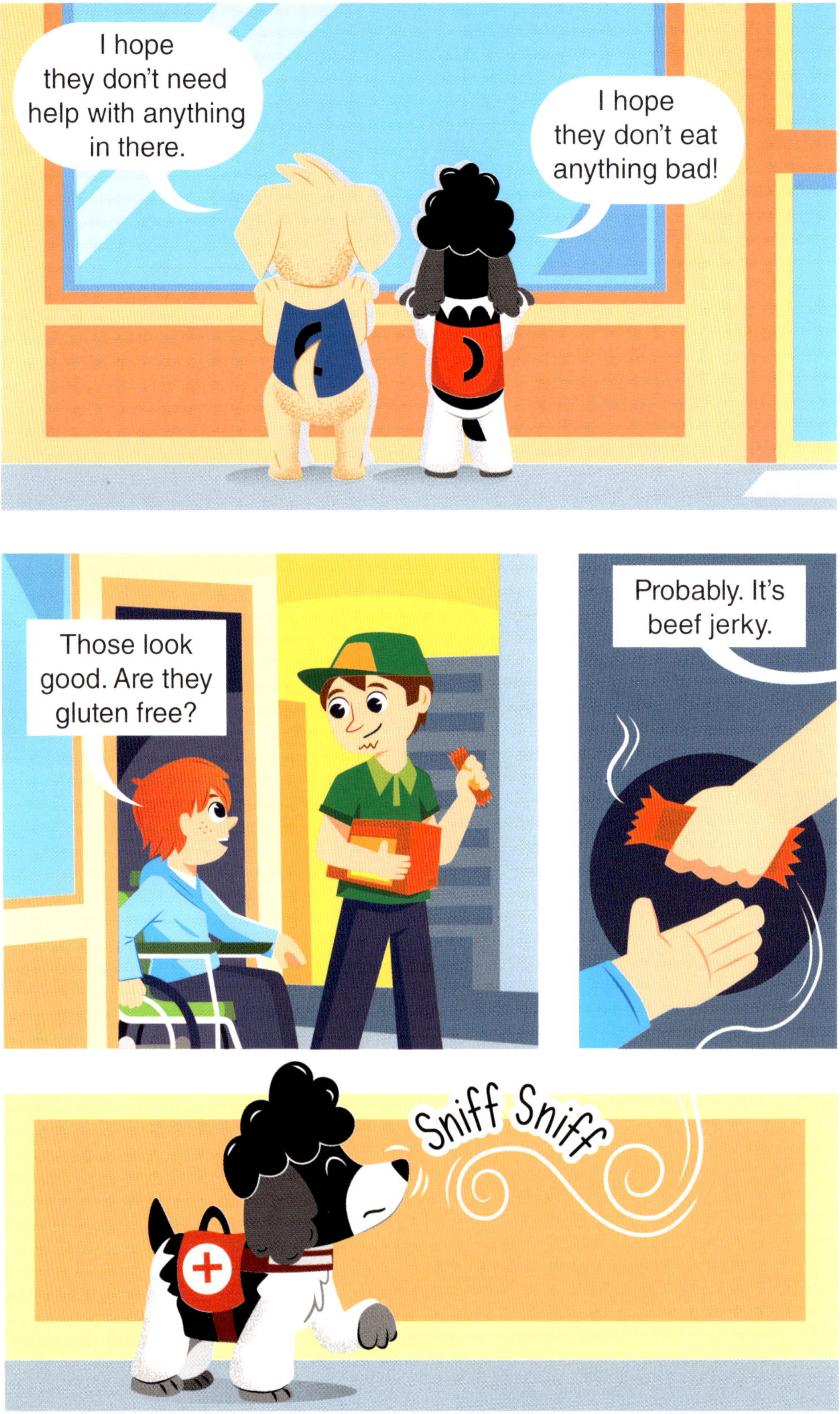
I hope they don't need help with anything in there.
I hope they don't eat anything bad!
Those look good. Are they gluten free?
Probably. It's beef jerky.
Sniff Sniff

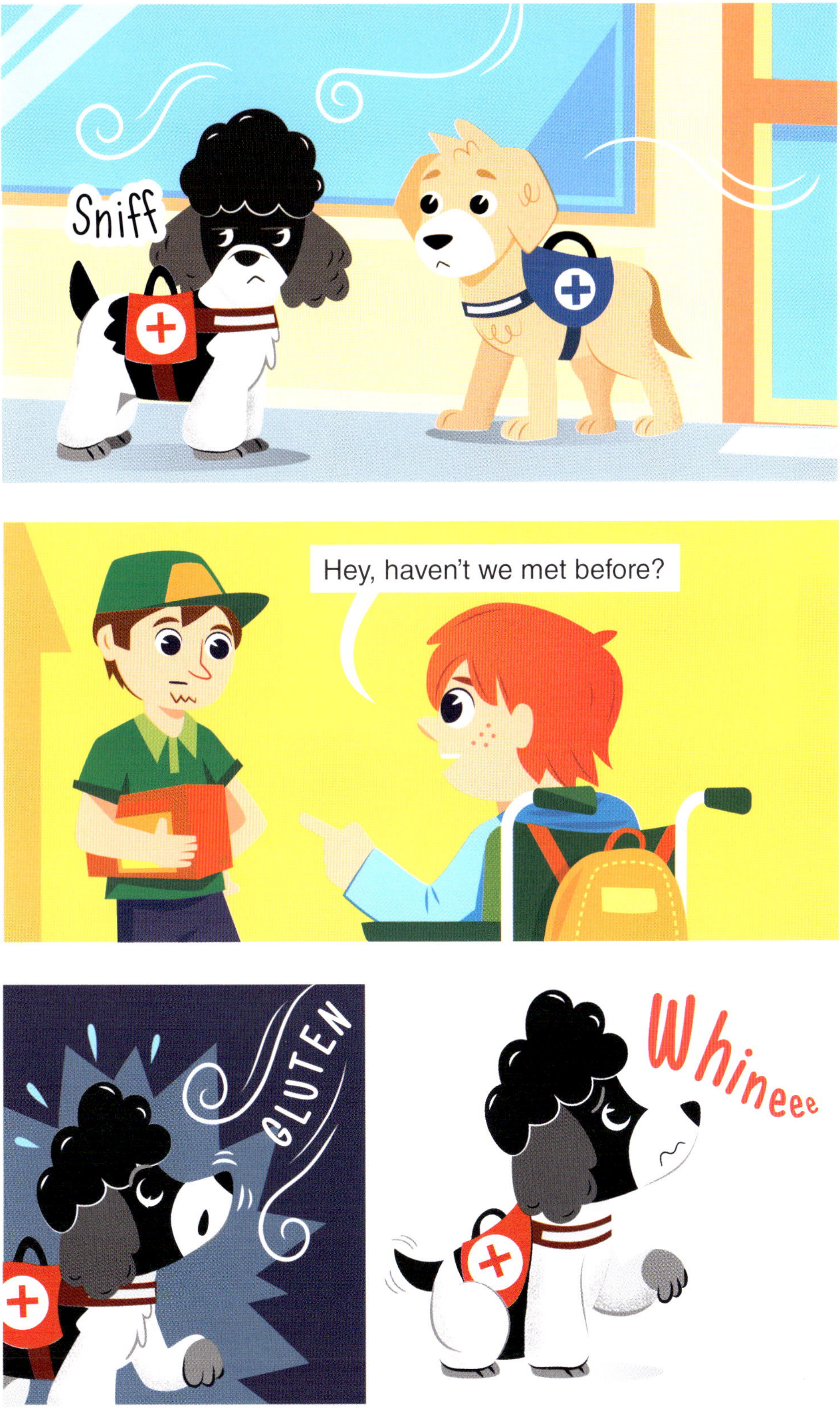
Sniff
Hey, haven't we met before?
GLUTEN
Whineee

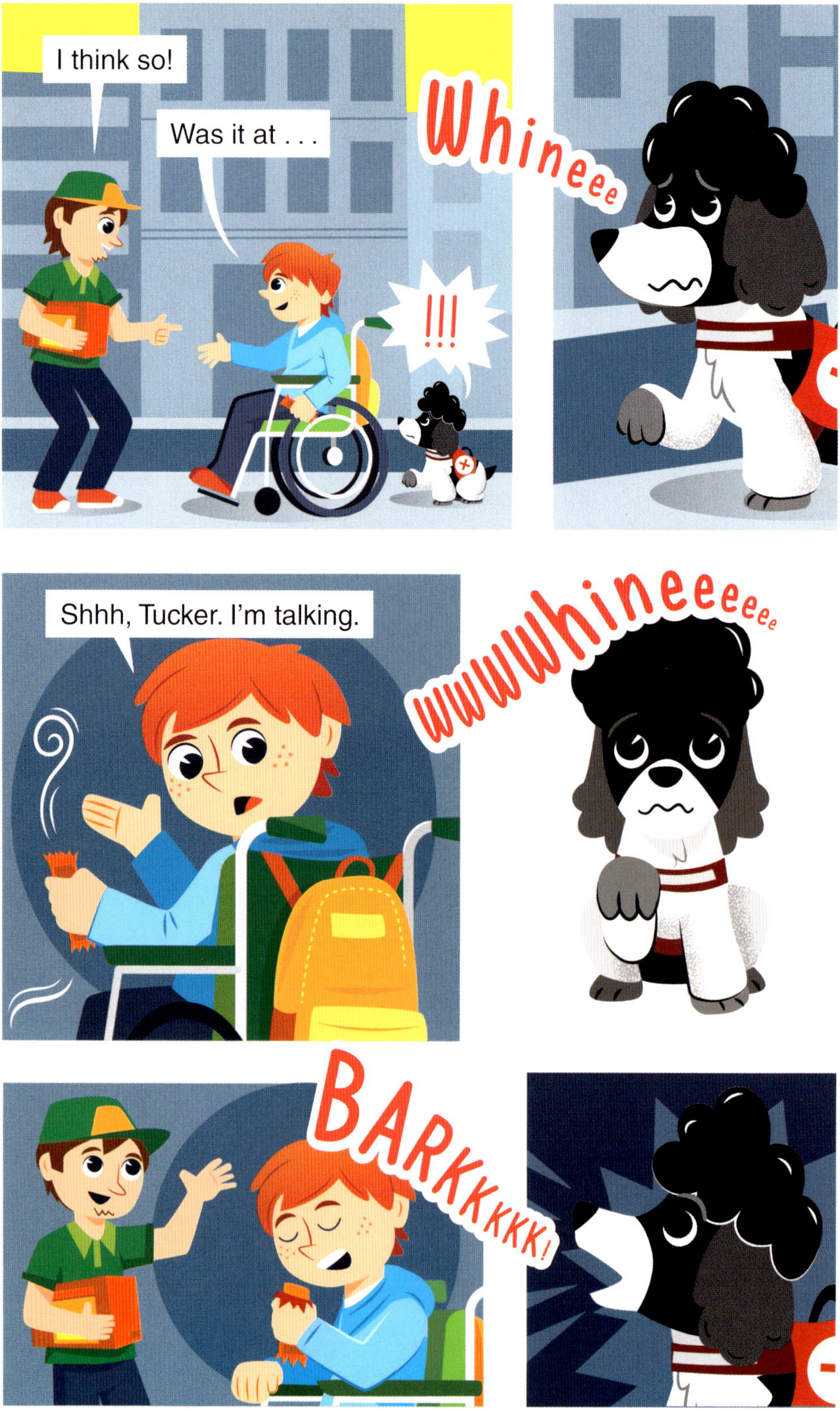
I think so!
Was it at . . .
!!!
Whineee
Shhh, Tucker. I'm talking.
wwwwhineeeeeee
BARKKKKK!

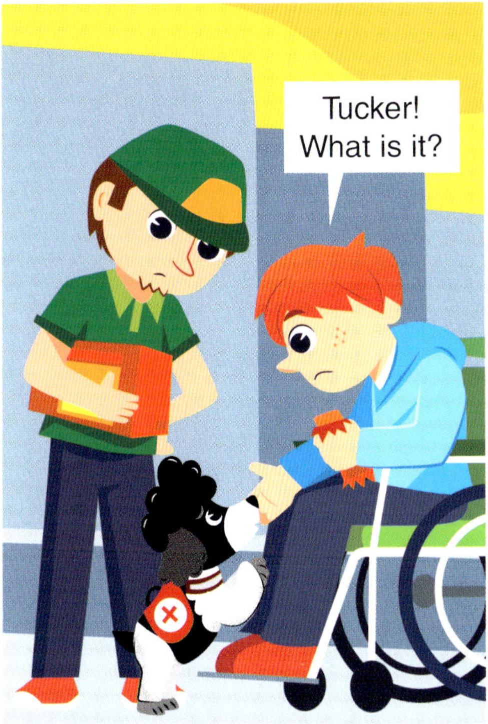
Tucker! What is it?

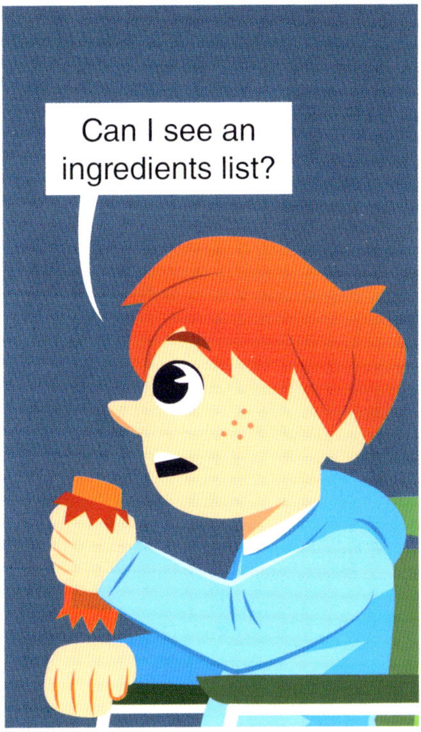
Can I see an ingredients list?

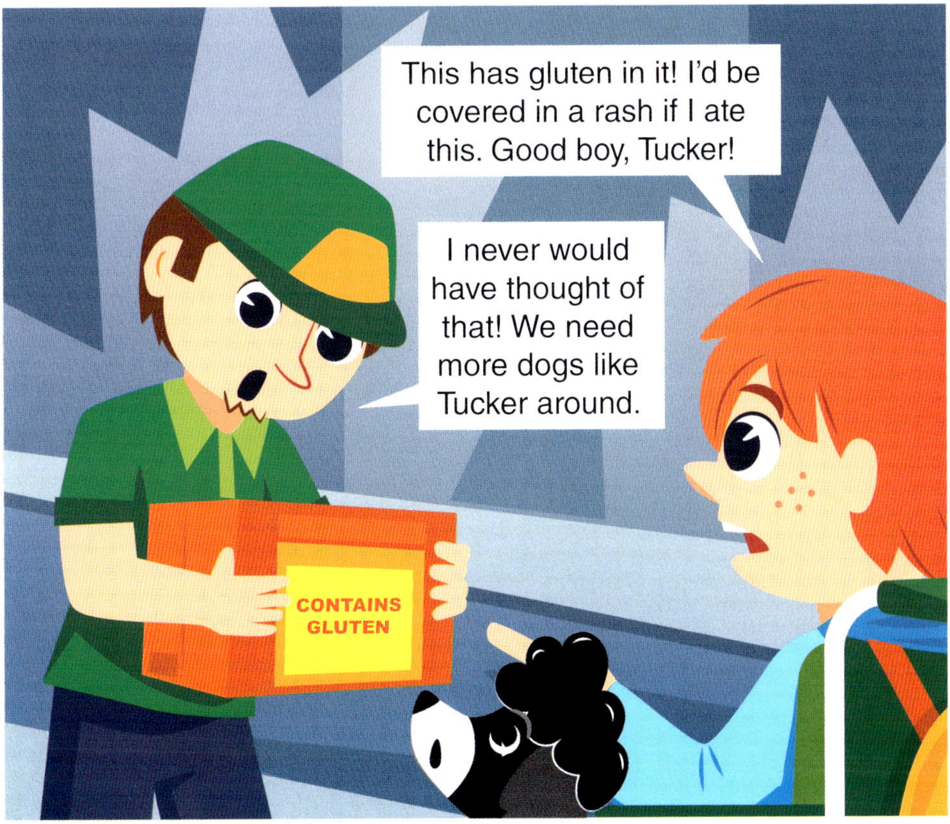
This has gluten in it! I'd be covered in a rash if I ate this. Good boy, Tucker!
I never would have thought of that! We need more dogs like Tucker around.
CONTAINS GLUTEN

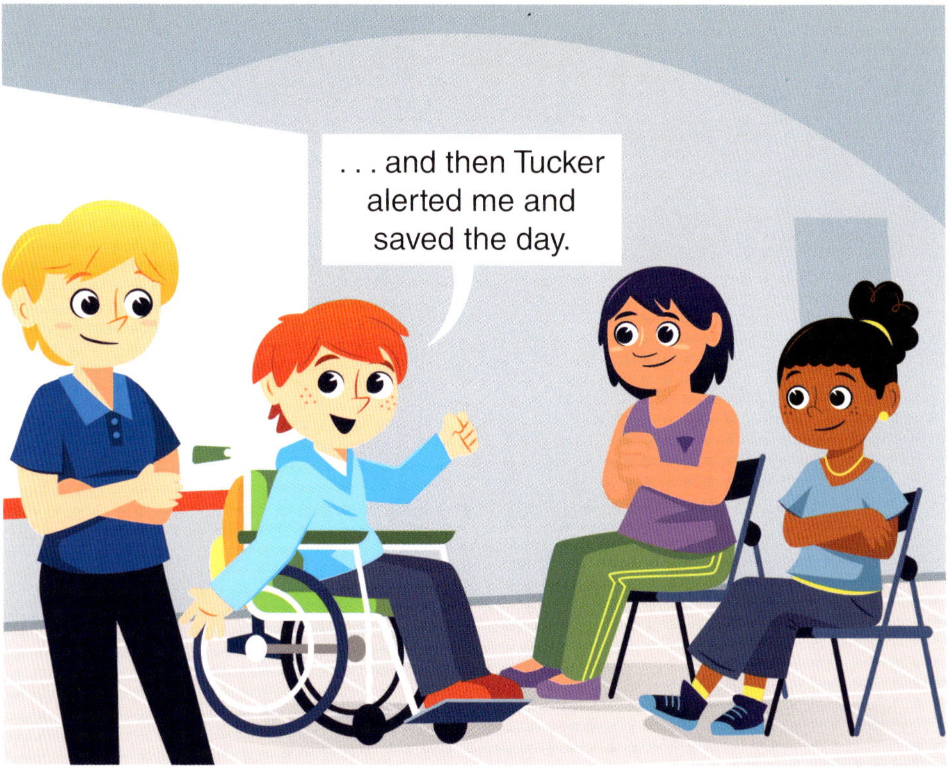
. . . and then Tucker
alerted me and
saved the day.

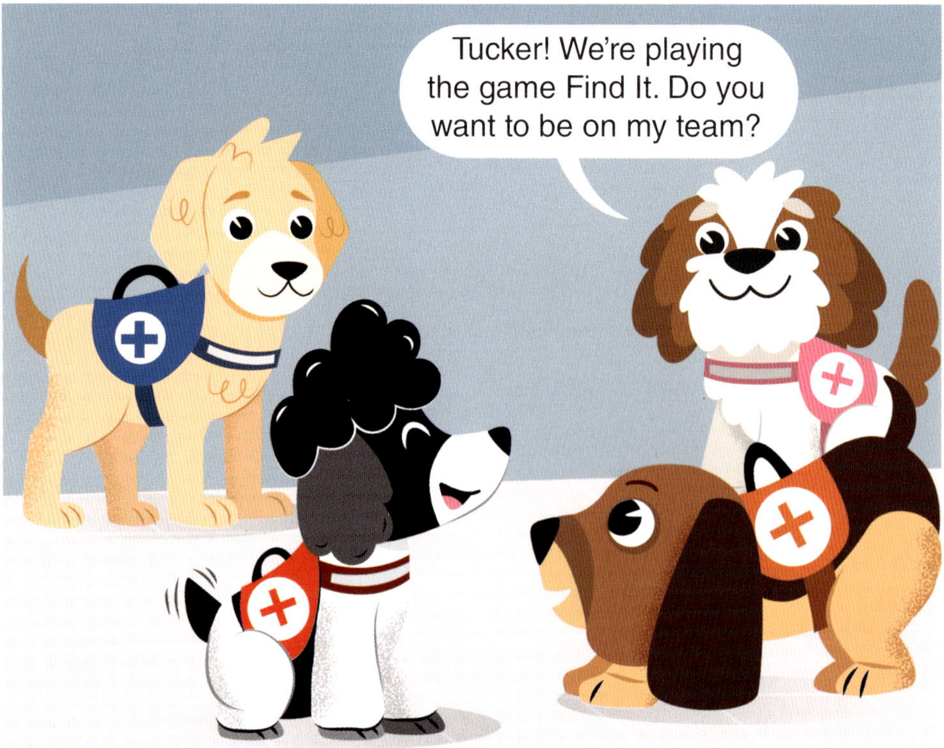
Tucker! We're playing
the game Find It. Do you
want to be on my team?

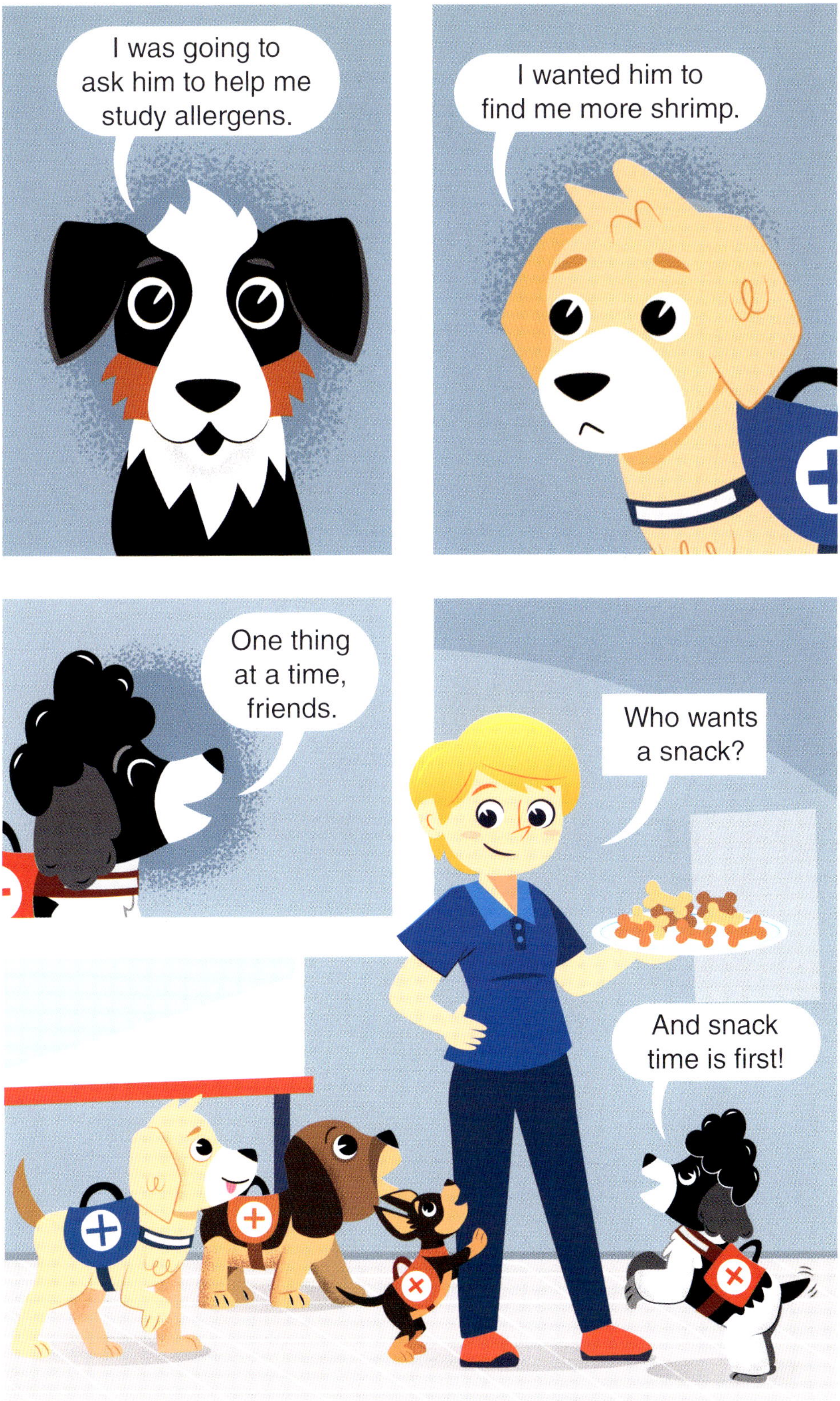
I was going to ask him to help me study allergens.
I wanted him to find me more shrimp.
One thing at a time, friends.
Who wants a snack?
And snack time is first!

Allergen Detection Dogs

Allergen detection dogs are trained to find things that would cause an allergic reaction in their person. They must have a very good sense of smell. They must also be able to find a single scent in a world full of smells.

The life of an allergen detection dog is like a life full of hide-and-seek! The dog looks around to find traces of the allergen. They might check foods before a meal. They could smell books, furniture, or even people. If they find the allergen, they alert their handler. They make sure the handler is not exposed to the allergen.

Good allergen detection dogs want to please their people. A good brain and the ability to be independent are good skills too. They must also be well behaved in public. Any dog can be trained to detect allergens. Hypoallergenic dogs, like poodles, are ideal for people who are allergic to dogs.

Thinking About the Story

1. Think about your favorite food. Look at the allergens list on page 12. Which of the most common allergens are in your favorite food? Were you surprised by any of them?

2. Pretend you are an allergen detection dog. Sit quietly and close your eyes. Take a deep breath. What can you smell? Do the smells become stronger when you focus on them?

3. Tucker works hard to learn his job. Why is it so important for Tucker to be trained correctly?

4. Having a food allergy can be tricky. What are some things you can do to include everyone when eating? What are some questions you could ask to make sure everyone feels included?

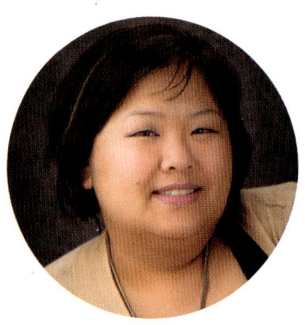

About the Author

Mari Bolte is an author and editor of children's books. She lives in southern Minnesota in a house in the woods. Dogs, cats, horses, and plenty of wildlife are always nearby. She has worked on books on all sorts of subjects, but animal books are always the best.

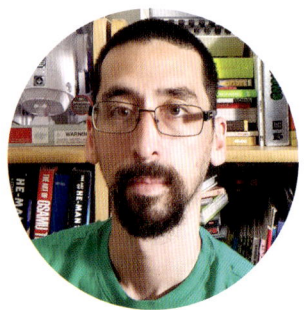

About the Illustrator

Diego Vaisberg is from Argentina. He is the DGPH Studio art director, working as designer and illustrator. He also works in the product and design department for Ink-co kids accessories brand and has been a professor in the Editorial design and Illustration Department at the Palermo University, Buenos Aires, since 2014.

Other Books in this Series

SERVICE PUPS in Training
DAPHNE SHOWS SUPPORT
An Emotional Support Dog Graphic Novel
K9 ACADEMY
written by Mari Bolte
illustrated by Alan Brown

SERVICE PUPS in Training
ELLIE'S BRAVE SEARCH
A Search and Rescue Dog Graphic Novel
K9 ACADEMY
written by Mari Bolte
illustrated by Diego Vaisberg

SERVICE PUPS in Training
ROSSI GUIDES THE WAY
A Guide Dog Graphic Novel
K9 ACADEMY
written by Mari Bolte
illustrated by Alan Brown

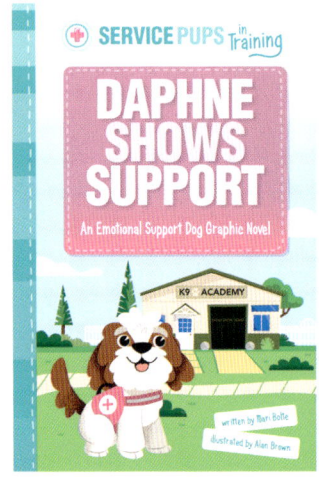

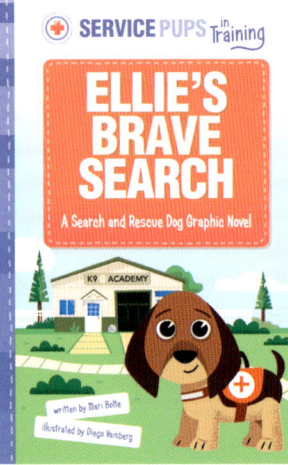

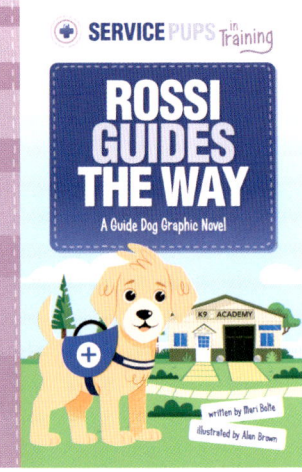